POPULAR
MUSIC

The Popular Music Series

Popular Music, 1920-1979 is a revised cumulation of and supersedes Volumes 1 through 8 of the *Popular Music* series, all of which are still in print:

Volume 1, 2nd ed., 1950-59	Volume 5, 1920-29
Volume 2, 1940-49	Volume 6, 1965-69
Volume 3, 1960-64	Volume 7, 1970-74
Volume 4, 1930-39	Volume 8, 1975-79

Published 1986:

Volume 9, 1980-84
Volume 10, 1985

Other Books by Bruce Pollock

In Their Own Words: Popular Songwriting, 1955-1974

The Face of Rock and Roll: Images of a Generation

When Rock Was Young: The Heyday of Top 40

When the Music Mattered: Rock in the 1960s

ISSN 0886-442X

VOLUME 10

1985

POPULAR MUSIC

An Annotated Guide to American Popular Songs,
Including Introductory Essay, Lyricists and Composers
Index, Important Performances Index, Awards Index,
and List of Publishers

BRUCE POLLOCK
Editor

GALE RESEARCH COMPANY
BOOK TOWER ● *DETROIT, MICHIGAN 48226*

Bruce Pollock, *Editor*
Thomas M. Bachmann, *Assistant Editor*
Marie A. Cruz, *Editorial Assistant*

Mary Beth Trimper, *Production Supervisor*
Darlene K. Maxey, *Production Assistant*
Arthur Chartow, *Art Director*

Dennis LaBeau, *Editorial Data Systems Director*
Theresa Rocklin, *Program Design*
Doris D. Goulart, *Editorial Data Entry Supervisor*
Jean Hinman Portfolio, *Editorial Data Entry Associate*
Sue Lynch, Mildred Sherman, Joyce M. Stone, *Senior Data Entry Assistants*

Frederick G. Ruffner, *Publisher*
Dedria Bryfonski, *Editorial Director*
Ellen T. Crowley, *Associate Editorial Director*
Linda S. Hubbard, *Senior Editor, Popular Music Series*

Computerized photocomposition by
Automatech Graphics
New York, New York

Printed in the United States of America

Contents

About the Book and How to Use It

This volume is the tenth of a series whose aim is to set down in permanent and practical form a selective, annotated list of the significant popular songs of our times. Other indexes of popular music have either dealt with special areas, such as jazz or theater and film music, or been concerned chiefly with songs that achieved a degree of popularity as measured by the music-business trade indicators, which vary widely in reliability.

New Annual Publication Schedule

The first nine volumes in the *Popular Music* series covered sixty-five years of song history in increments of five or ten years. Volume 10 initiates a new annual publication schedule, making background information available as soon as possible after a song achieves prominence. Yearly publication also allows deeper coverage—well over four hundred songs per year, instead of about three hundred, with additional details about writers' inspiration, uses of songs, album appearances, and more. (Songs with copyright dates before 1985 have full entries in this volume if not covered in the series before. Cross references lead to complete entries in earlier volumes for songs already prominent in previous years.)

Indexes Provide Additional Access

Three indexes make the valuable information in the song listings even more accessible to users. The Lyricists & Composers Index shows all the songs represented in *Popular Music, 1985,* that are credited to a given individual. The Important Performances Index (introduced in the revised cumulation, *Popular Music, 1920-1979)* tells at a glance what albums, musicals, films, television shows, or other media featured songs that are represented in the volume. The index is arranged by broad media category, then alphabetically by the show or album title, with the songs listed under each title. Finally, the Awards Index (also introduced in the cumulation) provides a list of the songs nominated for awards by the American Academy of Motion Picture Arts and Sciences (Academy

About the Book and How to Use It

Award) and the American Academy of Recording Arts and Sciences (Grammy Award). Winning songs are indicated by asterisks.

List of Publishers

The List of Publishers is an alphabetically arranged directory providing addresses for the publishers of the songs represented in this tenth volume of *Popular Music*. Also noted is the organization handling performance rights for the publisher—American Society of Composers, Authors, and Publishers (ASCAP) . . . Broadcast Music, Inc. (BMI) . . . or Society of European Stage Authors and Composers (SESAC).

Tracking Down Information on Songs

Unfortunately, the basic records kept by the active participants in the music business are often casual, inaccurate, and transitory. There is no single source of comprehensive information about popular songs, and those sources that do exist do not publish complete material about even the musical works with which they are directly concerned. Two of the primary proprietors of basic information about our popular music are the major performing rights societies—ASCAP and BMI. Although each of these organizations has considerable information about the songs of its own writer and publisher members and has also issued indexes of its own songs, their files and published indexes are designed primarily for clearance identification by the commercial users of music. Their publications of annual or periodic lists of their "hits" necessarily include only a small fraction of their songs, and the facts given about these are also limited. Both ASCAP and BMI are, however, invaluable and indispensable sources of data about popular music. It is just that their data and special knowledge are not readily accessible to the researcher.

Another basic source of information about musical compositions and their creators and publishers is the Copyright Office of the Library of Congress. There a computerized file lists each published, unpublished, republished, and renewed copyright of songs registered with the Office since 1979. This is helpful for determining the precise date of the declaration of the original ownership of musical works, but contains no other information. To complicate matters further, some authors, composers, and publishers have been known to employ rather makeshift methods of protecting their works legally, and there are songs listed in *Popular Music* that may not be found in the Library of Congress files.

Selection Criteria

In preparing this series, the editor was faced with a number of separate problems. The first and most important of these was that of selection. The stated aim of the project—to offer the user as comprehensive and accurate a listing of significant popular songs as possible—has been the guiding criterion. The purpose has never been to offer a judgment on the quality of any songs or to indulge a prejudice for or against any type of popular music. Rather, it is the purpose of *Popular Music* to document those musical works that (1) achieved a substantial degree of popular acceptance, (2) were exposed to the public in especially notable circumstances, or (3) were accepted and given important performances by influential musical and dramatic artists.

Another problem was whether or not to classify the songs as to type. Most works of music are subject to any number of interpretations and, although it is possible to describe a particular performance, it is more difficult to give a musical composition a label applicable not only to its origin but to its subsequent musical history. In fact, the most significant versions of some songs are often quite at variance with their origins. Citations for such songs in *Popular Music* indicate the important facts about not only their origins but also their subsequent lives, rather than assigning an arbitrary and possibly misleading label.

Research Sources

The principal sources of information for the titles, authors, composers, publishers, and dates of copyright of the songs in this volume were the Copyright Office of the Library of Congress, ASCAP, BMI, and individual writers and publishers. Data about best-selling recordings were obtained principally from two of the leading music business trade journals—*Billboard* and *Cash Box*. For the historical notes; information about foreign, folk, public domain, and classical origins; and identification of theatrical, film, and television introducers of songs, the editor relied upon collections of record album notes, theater programs, sheet music, newspaper and magazine articles, and other material, both his own and that in the Lincoln Center Library for the Performing Arts in New York City.

Contents of a Typical Entry

The primary listing for a song includes

- Title and alternate title(s)
- Country of origin (for non-U.S. songs)
- Author(s) and composer(s)

- Current publisher, copyright date
- Annotation on the song's origins or performance history

Title: The full title and alternate title or titles are given exactly as they appear on the Library of Congress copyright record or, in some cases, the sheet music. Since even a casual perusal of the book reveals considerable variation in spelling and punctuation, it should be noted that these are neither editorial nor typographical errors but the colloquialisms of the music trade. The title of a given song as it appears in this series is, in almost all instances, the one under which it is legally registered.

Foreign Origin: If the song is of foreign origin, the primary listing indicates the country of origin after the title. Additional information may be noted, such as the original title, copyright date, writer, publisher in country of origin, or other facts about the adaptation.

Authorship: In all cases, the primary listing reports the author or authors and the composer or composers. The reader may find variations in the spelling of a songwriter's name. This results from the fact that some writers used different forms of their names at different times or in connection with different songs. These variants appear in the Lyricists & Composers Index as well. In addition to this kind of variation in the spelling of writers' names, the reader will also notice that in some cases, where the writer is also the performer, the name as a writer may differ from the form of the name used as a performer.

Publisher: The current publisher is listed. Since *Popular Music* is designed as a practical reference work rather than an academic study, and since copyrights more than occasionally change hands, the current publisher is given instead of the original holder of the copyright. If a publisher has, for some reason, copyrighted a song more than once, the years of the significant copyright subsequent to the year of the original copyright are also listed after the publisher's name.

Annotation: The primary listing mentions significant details about the song's history—the musical, film, or other production in which the song was introduced or featured and, where important, by whom it was introduced, in the case of theater and film songs . . . any other performers identified with the song . . . first or best-selling recordings and album inclusions, indicating the performer and the record company . . . awards . . . and other relevant data. The name of a performer may be listed differently in connection with different songs, especially over a period of years. The name listed is the form of the name given in connection with a particular performance or record. It should be noted that the designation "best-selling record" does not mean that the record was a "hit." It means simply that the record or records noted as "best-selling" were the best-selling record or records of that particular song, in comparison with the sales of other records of the same song. Dates are provided for important recordings and performances.

Cross-References

Any alternate titles appearing in bold type after the main title in a primary listing are also cross-referenced in the song listings. If a song previously covered in the *Popular Music* series also attained prominence in 1985, the title and new achievement are noted here with a reference to the appropriate earlier volume.

Popular Music in 1985

Trends of protest and nostalgia, themes of sex and violence, and the demands of proliferating film and television productions combined to make 1985 a year of American song creation nearly unparalleled in history. This revival played out on several stages, not the least of which was the political arena in Washington, DC—site of so many marches and demonstrations back in the sixties, song's last such gleaming moment in the sun.

The Return of Social Concern

With an American songwriting renaissance in full flower, performers and bands occupied heartland stages, not only celebrating their own creations, but marking a national community coming together, inspired by mutually energizing music and causes. The momentum against African famine, initiated in Britain by Bob Geldof's "Do They Know It's Christmas" in 1984, crested with America's Lionel Richie-Michael Jackson anthem "We Are the World" and the simultaneous Live Aid concerts which were broadcast worldwide from London and Philadelphia. The success of Live Aid sparked benefits by performers across the musical spectrum for causes ranging from the economic crisis of U.S. farmers and the Mexican earthquake, to the epidemic of acquired immune deficiency syndrome (AIDS). Bruce Springsteen's charismatic commitment to a variety of social concerns and his former partner Steve Van Zandt's "Sun City" chant against South African apartheid set a tone for the year of high optimism, backed with a realistic, street-and-history toughened knowledge of the long haul.

Topping the year off with a sense of drama, perspective, and irony, Bob Dylan—a featured voice on "We Are the World" and a weathered and poignant presence at the Live Aid and Farm Aid concerts—released the astonishing five-record *Biograph* set. The albums collected three decades of achievement into one package and definitively proved Dylan the forefather of a generation still expanding, still preaching the surreal, jugular-piercing gospel he invented, perfected, and glorified. *Biograph* would be a much needed weapon, a soul-comforting Bible to grasp in the troubled atmosphere of threatened censorship that arose out of Washington.

Popular Music in 1985

In the capital a group formed by the wives of several members of the federal government demanded Congressional hearings on the lyrics of rock 'n' roll. The Parents Music Resource Center (PMRC) proposed a labelling system analagous to the "PG" (parental guidance suggested) used in the film industry as a way to protect adolescents from the suggestive words of popular records. Their testimony was challenged by that of such musicians as Frank Zappa, former leader of the legendary Mothers of Invention, and Dee Snider of the deliberately outrageous Twisted Sister. The drama of the hearings and the threat to the heart and soul of rock 'n' roll seemed to arouse many songwriters into producing their best work.

Love, Patriotism, and Other Themes

Closer to the middle of the road, pop music continued to perform its more traditional function as purveyor of platitudes, palliative to the masses, offering an abundance of love songs for throbbing hearts teenaged and older. These transitory odes had no greater purpose than to commemorate a time or a place, a chance encounter or a last embrace with a catchy tune and greeting-card poetics. Yet even these efforts exhibited a higher level of intelligence and intensity, etching the place more firmly in the consciousness, making the last embrace all the more sensuous for its finality. Sophistication in setting and emotion enhanced the work of stock players and packaged teen idols.

George Michael's efforts with Wham!, "Careless Whisper" and "Wake Me Up Before You Go Go," respectively the number one and number three songs of the year according to *Billboard* magazine, evinced a nightclub chic worlds removed from the discos of Brooklyn popularized by the Bee Gees, John Travolta, and the movie *Saturday Night Fever* in the previous decade. The torchy tramp portrayed by Madonna and scripted by the writers of her hits "Like a Virgin" (Tom Kelly and Billy Steinberg) and "Crazy for You" (John Bettis and Jon Lind) was a quantum leap in sleaze-tease quotient and in witty self-knowledge beyond any number of girl-as-victim, singer-as-puppet, and woman-as-loser songs of the past thirty years. In "I Want to Know What Love Is" Mick Jones, surely one of rock's consummate craftsmen, dared to ask a question most of his dutifully resigned contemporaries would have preferred not to contemplate, even as they earned their livings batting out tepid soap operatic approximations.

Throughout the rest of the year's most honored and best-selling songs, themes of pride and confidence range across a terrain sprinkled with three-minute epitomes of philosophizing, psychological insight, political fury, sexual heat, sociological snippets, and just plain unbridled ebullience. The convergence of the nationalism promoted by the Reagan administration, the 1984 Olympics in Los Angeles, and such pop culture icons as actor Sylvestor Stallone's *Rambo,* with the musical influence of Bruce Springsteen's landmark 1984 album, *Born in the U.S.A.,* continued to shape popular songs from John Cougar Mellencamp's "Small Town" to Charlie Daniels's "Amber Waves of Grain." Even commercials caught the beat, exemplified by the revitalized Chrysler Corporation's slogan, "The pride is back, born in America." An apt credo for a patriotic year, even though a blatant ripoff on a neo-Springsteenian theme. So it goes.

While these songs were designed to draw enthusiastic agreement, others—intentionally or not—drew criticism. Gays alleged that Mark Knopfler's "Money for Nothing" was a slur. Others took offense at Prince's graphic description of female anatomy in "Sugar Walls," given steamy life by Sheena Easton . . . or at Madonna's enthusiastic acceptance of greed—a sore point in a year of Yuppies—in "Material Girl". . . or at David Lee Roth's sexist interpretation of the Beach Boys' classic "California Girls." Many more, however, were moved by Lionel Richie's tribute to the late Marvin Gaye, "Missing You," as sung by Diana Ross, or by "Nightshift," a tune from Lionel's old group, the Commodores, in which they honored Gaye and Jackie Wilson as well. Those on the side of sentiment couldn't help but applaud the success of Julian Lennon, son of the murdered former Beatle, when "Valotte" and "Too Late for Goodbyes" were released on these shores. "We Built This City" by the Starship (formerly Jefferson Starship) inspired some to proclaim a restoration of the long missing power of rock. Other writers demonstrated that power in different ways. Corey Hart's "Never Surrender," John Parr's "St. Elmo's Fire (Man in Motion)," "We Belong," by Pat Benatar, and "Everybody Wants to Rule the World," by Tears for Fears, all espoused a more personal credo of self-realization by ordeal, a coming of age through psychic growth. And, you could dance to them.

Songs from Films

As usual, movie assignments, holding the possibility of the venerable Academy Award rather than the more common Grammy and sometimes offering superior inspiration from the material being filmed, prompted songwriters to some of the finest efforts of the year. Although "St. Elmo's Fire (Man in Motion)," by John Parr and David Foster, inexplicably failed to gain a nomination, Stephen Bishop, a vocalist for "It Might Be You," the theme from *Tootsie* nominated in 1982, returned to the circle of the nominees, as a writer, with "Separate Lives" from

White Nights. "Say You, Say Me," from the same film (and not a musical, at that) earned Lionel Richie one of his two nominations, the other coming for "Miss Celie's Blues (Sisters)," which he wrote with Rod Temperton and Quincy Jones for *The Color Purple.* "The Power of Love," from *Back to the Future,* was a smash for Huey Lewis & The News, as well as drawing an Oscar nomination. "Surprise, Surprise" was added to the score of the film version of the Broadway musical *A Chorus Line* by writers Hamlisch and Kleban especially to secure a nomination as best original song. It did—surprise, surprise.

Although this completes the list of Academy Award nominees, it by no means defines the extent of quality songs debuting in movie sound-tracks in 1985. At least a dozen tunes ascended to the upper reaches of the pop charts, propelled by the multi-media boost only a feature-length movie showcase (with the requisite music video trailer) can provide. *Beverly Hills Cop* had three such tunes: "The Heat Is On," "Neutron Dance," and "Axel F." In addition to "The Power of Love," "St. Elmo's Fire," and "Separate Lives," these movie songs hit the top of the pops: "Don't You Forget about Me," from *The Breakfast Club;* "Rhythm of the Night," from *The Last Dragon;* "That's What Friends Are For," originally used in the 1982 flick *Nightshift;* and Bryan Adams's re-released "Heaven," which premiered in *A Night in Heaven.* The rock group Duran Duran contributed its first soundtrack for the James Bond spy movie *A View to a Kill,* while Tina Turner had a featured role in the futuristic fantasy *Mad Max Beyond Thunderdome,* for which she also recorded "We Don't Need Another Hero."

Songs on Television

Lacking Hollywood's diversity, the primary contribution of the small screen—television—to popular music remained its showcasing of music videos, both on special all-music cable channels like MTV (Music Television) for rock and VH1 (Video Hits One) for adult contemporary songs and on weekly shows on network and independent stations. However, one series, not ostensibly a music show, emerged as virtually a sixty-minute slot for a rock 'n' roll soundtrack each week. *Miami Vice* did, in fact, yield a hit album in 1985. This highly glamorized detective show revived certain rock chestnuts, notably "In the Air Tonight," by Phil Collins. More obscure items integrated into the action took on a cachet not unlike that proferred by *Saturday Night Live* in its heyday. Prime-time exposure boosted hit singles twenty to thirty points on the *Billboard, Cash Box,* and *Variety* charts, as the Monkees and the Partridge Family had learned all too well when they had weekly shows in an earlier decade. *Miami Vice* went the situation comedies of the sixties one better in its marriage of television and song, however. Glenn Frey's song "Smuggler's Blues" was the basis for an entire episode of the show, with Frey himself as a featured character. This use recalled the film version of Arlo Guthrie's picaresque ballad "Alice's Restaurant" in the late sixties and the album, rock opera, film, and ballet appearances of the Who's *Tommy*. Frey was just one of many stars who made appearances on *Miami Vice*, but his was successful enough that the producers succumbed to the characteristic drive of television moguls to make too much of a good thing and they brought him back a second time. The show's two-hour premier episode in the fall of 1985 featured Frey's debut of his song "You Belong to the City." It had no trouble cracking radio play lists nationwide.

Theatrical Songs

Unfortunately, Broadway and its legendary local commodity, musical theater, had no such luck and apparently little intent to mine the music video format so successfully exploited by television and films. This despite the fact that two of its more successful endeavors of the year were composed by writers who had previously had Top 40 songs. Rupert Holmes ("The Pina Colada Song") wrote *The Mystery of Edwin Drood*, based on an unfinished Charles Dickens novel. Roger Miller ("King of the Road") was the country bumpkin who turned Mark Twain's *Huckleberry Finn* into *Big River*. Other than these two admittedly less-than-sensational productions, Broadway had little material to make into a music video. Andrew Lloyd Webber's *Song and Dance* rehashed old material. Charles Strouse's *Mayor* was a topical revue of interest to the fans and foes of Ed Koch, but unlikely to have much appeal outside the New York City area. Masterly Stephen Sondheim had no new material produced, but was represented by two monumental album releases. A four-record boxed set reprising his career was, for another audience, an event on a par with Dylan's release of *Biograph*. Fans of the musical also appreciated the all-star concert recording of Sondheim's 1972 classic score, *Follies*. The composer also contributed a rewrite of his "Putting It Together" to Barbara Streisand's long awaited and very successful *Broadway Album*.

Perhaps the most intriguing project cooking these days in the realm of the musical is one that did exploit the music video concept. Authors Tim Rice (who has been the hit single route before, with "Jesus Christ, Superstar" and "I Don't Know How to Love Him" from his musical *Jesus Christ, Superstar)* and Benny Anderson and Bjorn Ulvaeus (the male half of the Swedish supergroup ABBA) found they had a hit U.S. single with "One Night in Bangkok" from *Chess* well before the show even opened in its native England. The exotic imagery of the video for the song may have boosted its appeal and whetted appetites for the entire musical. Perhaps other Broadway producers will consider this marketing device in the future.

Rhythm 'n' Blues, Country, and Folk Songs

Although both rhythm 'n' blues (also known as black music or dance music) and country music must be counted as forbears of today's popular music, they differ greatly in how they are relating to mainstream music just now. The most popular black musicians are also the most popular music makers and songwriters for a general audience. Lionel Richie, Stevie Wonder, Ashford and Simpson, Bobby Womack, Sade, Kool & The Gang, Prince, Billy Ocean, the Pointer Sisters—all project a universal style that transcends genre. Moreover, the subject matter of rhythm 'n' blues—the many manifestations of sexual adrenalin—only ensures the timelessness of the message, while the sass and pizazz of the dance club, with new songs issued as fast as new steps are created and new catch phrases ushered into the slanguage of the street, give the music a drive and urgency that attracts artists of different hues. Most dance hits emanate from independent record companies, confirming the grassroots nature of this genre, the hot-off-the-presses aspect of the territory, where the music strikes the body first, before it gets civilized into the button-down brain of pop. Where else but on the r 'n' b side could you come up with 1985's two local favorites that made it nationwide (Rocking Sidney's "My Toot Toot" from Louisiana and "Roxanne, Roxanne" from the streets of New York City)?

The country heritage of rock 'n' roll extends just as far back and just as deep. Hank Williams inspired Bob Dylan. Buddy Holly, Carl Perkins, Elvis Presley, Johnny Cash, and Jerry Lee Lewis are major rockabilly influences still felt three decades later. What did Tin Pan Alley ever have that Tennessee's Felice and Boudleaux Bryant didn't? Yet in 1985 country music was a virtual world unto itself, symbolized by Ronnie Milsap's best-selling "Lost in the Fifties." The country neighborhood this year is a place we've been to many times before, the candy store still selling baseball cards of the Brooklyn Dodgers. Unfailingly realistic, if not downright depressing in their lyrical concerns, country songwriters continue to churn out titles like these: "Drinkin' and Dreamin'," "She's Single Again," "Some Fools Never Learn," "Meet Me in Montana," "She Keeps the Home Fires Burning." Content to grow old with their audiences, established country musicians are giving away the turf to rock-inspired newcomers like the Long Ryders, Green on Red, R.E.M., Jason & The Scorchers, and the Dream Syndicate. These groups have also rediscovered the folk sensibility till now buried on the dirt roads of the sixties.

Some of the best songs written in 1985 come out of this latent sensibility. Suzanne Vega released an album chock full of them: "Freeze Tag," "Small Blue Thing," "Marlene on the Wall," and others. Vega is a graduate of Barnard College at Columbia University and an alumna, if you will, of the *Fast Folk Musical Magazine*, a recorded periodical that gives voice to a community still dedicated to practicing the fine art of the folk song. Bob Franke's devastating "For Real" also comes from this tradition. Other evidence of its persistence is the Roches' rendition of Mark Johnson's ethereal "Love Radiates Around." Richard and Linda Thompson, once the king and queen of folk music, now patrol individual domains. Richard's "She Twists the Knife Again" and Linda's "One Clear Moment" give adequate testimony to the mastery they both maintain. The Los Angeles folk scene produced "Song for the Dreamers," written by Dan Stuart and Steve Wynn. Finally, Dylan's *Biograph* set unearthed enough treasures to keep folk fans occupied through the millennium, among them the legendary "Percy's Song" and the equally historic "I'll Keep It with Mine."

Other songwriters mined different veins of experience to produce quality material, ranging from the gritty wordplay of John Hiatt ("She Said the Same Thing to Me") to the other worldly chants of Kate Bush ("Running Up That Hill"). Marshall Crenshaw continued to refine his minimalist approach with "Little Wild One," while Paul Westerberg of the Replacements had to maximize his talents for big label bucks now in hand. His efforts yielded "Here Comes a Regular" and the quirky "Swingin' Party." After writing for Cyndi Lauper in 1984, Eric Bazilian and Rob Hyman put out their own album as the Hooters, featuring pungent and resounding works like "Where Do the Children Go." Talking Heads' David Byrne was at his most accessible in "And She Was." From television's *Saturday Night Live*, musician Paul Shaffer— whose "Honey (Touch Me with My Clothes On)" with SNL veteran Gilda Radner remains one of the best love songs ever—assisted comedian Billy Crystal with "You Look Marvelous," one of his funniest efforts. And, last of all, old Lonesome Don Henley, formerly of the Eagles, gave us perhaps the year's best song, "The Boys of Summer." Oddly enough, this anguished and totally real ballad managed to hit the top of the charts and received two Grammy nominations.

We could well be on the brink of another Golden Age. Tune in next year.

—Bruce Pollock

POPULAR
MUSIC

A

After the Fire (English)
Words and music by Peter Townshend.
Eel Pie Music, England, 1985/Atlantic Recording Corp., England, 1985/Bejubop, England, 1985.
Best-selling record by Roger Daltrey from the album *Under a Raging Moon* (Atlantic, 85).

Ain't No Road Too Long
Words and music by Waylon Jennings.
Waylon Jennings Music, 1985.
Introduced by Waylon Jennings and the Seseme Street muppet character Big Bird in the film *Follow That Bird.*

Ain't She Something Else
Words and music by Jerry Foster and Bill Rice.
Jack & Bill Music Co., 1985.
Best-selling record by Conway Twitty from the album *Don't Call Him a Cowboy* (Warner Bros., 85).

Alive and Kicking (English)
Words and music by Simple Minds.
Colgems-EMI Music Inc., 1985.
Best-selling record by Simple Minds from the album *Once Upon a Time* (A & M/Virgin, 85).

All I Need
Words and music by Cliff Magness, Glen Ballard, and David Pack.
Yellow Brick Road Music, 1984/MCA, Inc./Art Street Music.
Best-selling record by Jack Wagner from the album *All I Need* (Warner Bros., 85).

All She Wants to Do Is Dance
Words and music by Danny Kortchmar.
Kortchmar Music, 1984.
Best-selling record by Don Henley from the album *Building the Perfect Beast* (Warner Bros., 85).

All Through the Night
See *Popular Music, 1980-1984.*

All You Zombies
Words and music by Rob Hyman and Eric Bazilian.
Dub Notes, 1982/Human Boy Music, 1982.
Best-selling record by The Hooters from the album *Nervous Night* (Columbia, 85).

Along Comes a Woman
Words and music by Peter Cetera and Mark Goldenberg.
Double Virgo Music, 1984/Music Corp. of America/Fleedleedee Music.
Best-selling record by Chicago from the album *Chicago XVII* (Warner Bros., 85).

Amber Waves of Grain
Words and music by Merle Haggard and Freddy Powers.
Mount Shasta Music Inc., 1985.
Introduced by Merle Haggard on the album *Amber Waves of Grain* (Epic, 85). Song deals with plight of the American farmer.

America Is
Words by Hal David, music by Joe Raposo.
Casa David, 1985/Jonico Music Inc.
Introduced by B. J. Thomas. The song was written for the centennial of the Statue of Liberty.

And She Was
Words and music by David Byrne, music by Chris Frantz, Tina Weymouth, and Jerry Harrison.
Index Music, 1985/Bleu Disque Music, 1985.
Introduced by The Talking Heads on the album *Little Creatures* (Sire, 85).

And We Danced
Words and music by Rob Hyman and Eric Bazilian.
Human Boy Music, 1984/Dub Notes.
Introduced by The Hooters on the album *Nervous Night* (Columbia, 85).

Angel
Words and music by Madonna and Steve Bray.
WB Music Corp., 1984/Bleu Disque Music/Webo Girl Music/WB
   Music Corp./Black Lion.
Best-selling record by Madonna in 1985 from the album *Like a Virgin*
   (Warner Bros., 84).

Appetite (Irish)
Words and music by Paddy McAloon.
Blackwood Music Inc., 1985.
Introduced by by Prefab Sprout on the album *Two Wheels Good* (Epic,
   85).

The Arbiter (I Know the Score) (English)
Words and music by Tim Rice, Bennie Andersson, and Bjorn
   Ulvaeus.
MCA, Inc., 1985.
Introduced by Bjorn Skifs (RCA, 85). From the musical *Chess,* due to
   open in England in 1986.

As Long as We Got Each Other
Words by John Bettis, music by Steven Dorff.
Oil Slick Music, 1985/Dorff Songs, 1985/John Bettis Music, 1985.
Introduced by B. J. Thomas on the television series *Growing Pains* (85).

Attack Me with Your Love
Words and music by Larry Blackmon and Kevin Kendricks.
All Seeing Eye Music, 1985/Larry Junior Music, 1985/King
   Kendrick Publishing, 1985.
Best-selling record by Cameo from the album *Single Life* (Polygram, 85).

Axel F
Music by Harold Faltermeyer.
Famous Music Corp., 1985.
Introduced in the film *Beverly Hills Cop* (85). Best-selling record by
   Harold Faltermeyer (MCA, 85).

B

Baby Bye Bye
Words and music by Gary Morris and James Brantley.
WB Music Corp., 1984/Gary Morris Music, 1984.
Best-selling record by Gary Morris from the album *Anything Goes* (Warner Bros., 85).

Baby, It's the Little Things, also known as **Little Things**
Words and music by Bill Barber.
Reynsong Music, 1985.
Best-selling record by The Oak Ridge Boys from the album *Step on Out* (MCA, 85).

Baby's Got Her Blue Jeans On
Words and music by Bob McDill.
Hall-Clement Publications, 1984.
Best-selling record by Mel McDaniel from the album *Let It Roll* (Capitol, 85). Nominated for a National Academy of Recording Arts and Sciences Award, Country Song of the Year, 1985.

Back in Stride
Words and music by Frankie Beverly.
Amazement Music, 1985.
Best-selling record by Maze featuring Frankie Beverly from the album *Can't Stop the Love* (Capitol, 85).

Be Near Me (English)
Words and music by Martin Fry and Mark White.
10 Music Ltd., England, 1985/Neutron Music, England, 1985/ Nymph Music, 1985.
Best-selling record by ABC from the album *How to Be a Billionaire* (Polygram, 85).

Be Your Man
Words and music by Jesse Johnson.
Almo Music Corp., 1985/Crazy People Music .

Best-selling record by Jesse Johnson's Revue from the album *Jesse Johnson's Revue* (A & M, 85).

The Beast in Me
Words and music by Eric Kaz and Marvin Morrow.
April Music, Inc., 1985/Kaz Music Co., 1985.
Introduced by The Pointer Sisters in the film *Heavenly Bodies* (85).

Beat of a Heart
Words and music by Zack Smith, Patty Smyth, and Keith Mack.
Blackwood Music Inc., 1984/Keishmack Music.
Best-selling record by Scandal featuring Patty Smyth in 1985 from the album *Warrior* (Columbia, 84).

Beep a Freak
Words and music by R. Taylor, Lonnie Simmons, and C. Wilson.
Temp Co., 1985.
Best-selling record by The Gap Band from the album *Gap Band VI* (RCA, 85).

Between Blue Eyes and Jeans
Words and music by Kenneth McDuffie.
Hall-Clement Publications, 1984.
Best-selling record by Conway Twitty from the album *Don't Call Him a Cowboy* (Warner Bros., 85).

The Big Sky (English)
Words and music by Kate Bush.
Screen Gems-EMI Music Inc., 1985.
Introduced by Kate Bush on the album *Hounds of Love* (EMI-America, 85).

Bigger Stones
Words and music by Paul Kamanski.
Paul Kamanski Music, 1985.
Best-selling record by The Beat Farmers from the album *Tales of the New West* (Rhino, 85).

Bit by Bit (Theme from *Fletch*)
Words by Frannie Golde, music by Harold Faltermeyer.
MCA, Inc., 1985/Franne Golde Music Inc., 1985/Rightsong Music Inc., 1985/Kilauea Music, 1985.
Best-selling record by Stephanie Mills (MCA, 85). Introduced in the film *Fletch* (85).

Blues Is King
Words and music by Marshall Crenshaw.
Colgems-EMI Music Inc., 1985/House of Greed Music, 1985.

Introduced by Marshall Crenshaw on the album *Downtown* (Warner Bros., 85).

Bop
Words and music by Jennifer Kimball and Paul Davis.
Michael H. Goldsen, Inc., 1985/Web 4 Music Inc., 1985/Sweet Angel Music, 1985.
Best-selling record by Dan Seals from the album *Won't Be Blue Anymore* (EMI-America, 85).

Born in the U.S.A.
See *Popular Music, 1980-1984*. Nominated for a National Academy of Recording Arts and Sciences Award, Record of the Year, 1985.

The Bottomless Lake
Words and music by John Prine.
Big Ears Music Inc., 1979/Bruised Oranges, 1979.
Introduced by John Prine on the album *Aimless Love* (Oh Boy, 85).

The Boys of Summer
Words and music by Don Henley and Mike Campbell.
Cass County Music Co., 1984/Wild Gator Music.
Best-selling record by Don Henley from the album *Building the Perfect Beast* (Warner Bros., 85). Nominated for National Academy of Recording Arts and Sciences Awards, Record of the Year, 1985, and Song of the Year, 1985.

Breakaway
Words and music by Jackie DeShannon and Sharon Sheeley.
CBS Unart Catalog Inc., 1983.
Introduced by Gail Davies in the film *Sylvester*.

Broken Wings
Words and music by Richard Page, Steven George, and John Lang.
Warner-Tamerlane Publishing Corp., 1985/Entente Music, 1985.
Best-selling record by Mr. Mister from the album *Welcome to the Real World* (RCA, 85).

Brothers in Arms (English)
Words and music by Mark Knopfler.
Chariscourt Ltd., 1985/Almo Music Corp., 1985/Virgin Music Ltd., 1985.
Introduced by Dire Straits on the album *Brothers in Arms* (Warner Bros., 85).

Burning Heart
Words and music by Frankie Sullivan and Jim Peterik.
Holy Moley Music, 1985/Rude Music, 1985/WB Music Corp., 1985/

Easy Action Music, 1985.
Best-selling record by Survivor (Scotti Bros., 85). Introduced in the film
  Rocky IV.

C

C-I-T-Y
Words and music by John Cafferty.
John Cafferty Music, 1985.
Best-selling record by John Cafferty and The Beaver Brown Band from
   the album *Tough All Over* (Scotti Bros., 85).

California Girls
Revived by David Lee Roth on the album *Crazy from the Heat* (Warner
   Bros., 85). See *Popular Music, 1920-1979.*

Call Me
Words and music by Peter Cox and Richie Drummie.
ATV Music Corp., 1985.
Introduced by Go West on the album *Go West* (Chrysalis, 85).

Call Me Mr. Telephone
Words and music by T. Carrasco.
Copyright Control, 1985.
Best-selling record by Cheyne (MCA, 85).

Call to the Heart
Words and music by Gregg Guiffria and David Eisley.
Kid Bird Music, 1984/Herds of Birds Music Inc., 1984/Greg
   Guiffria Music, 1984/Frozen Flame Music, 1984.
Best-selling record by Guiffria from the album *Guiffria* (MCA, 85).

Can You Help Me
Words and music by Jesse Johnson.
Almo Music Corp., 1985/Crazy People Music/Almo Music Corp.,
   1985.
Best-selling record by Jesse Johnson's Revue from the album *Jesse John-
   son's Revue* (A & M, 85).

Can't Fight This Feeling
Words and music by Kevin Cronin.

Fate Music, 1984.
Best-selling record by REO Speedwagon from the album *Wheels Are Turning* (Epic, 85).

Can't Get There from Here
Words and music by William Berry, Peter Buck, Mike Mills, and John Stipe.
Unichappell Music Inc., 1985.
Best-selling record by R.E.M. from the album *Fables of the Reconstruction* (I.R.S., 85).

Can't Keep a Good Man Down
Words and music by Robert Corbini.
Sabal Music, Inc., 1984.
Best-selling record by Alabama from the album *40 Hour Week* (RCA, 85).

Can't Stop the Girl (English)
Words and music by Linda Thompson.
Linda Thompson, England, 1985/Firesign Music Ltd., England, 1985/Chappell & Co., Inc., 1985.
Best-selling record by Linda Thompson from the album *One Clear Moment* (Warner Bros., 85).

Caravan of Love
Words and music by Earnest Isley, Marvin Isley, and Christopher Jasper.
April Music, Inc., 1985/IJI, 1985.
Best-selling record by Isley/Jasper/Isley from the album *Caravan of Love* (CBS Associated, 85).

Careless Whisper (English)
Words and music by George Michael and Andrew Ridgeley.
Chappell & Co., Inc., 1984.
Best-selling record by Wham! featuring George Michael, from the album *Make It Big* (Columbia, 84).

Centerfield
Words and music by John Fogerty.
Wenaha Music Co., 1984.
Best-selling record by John Fogerty from the album *Centerfield* (Warner Bros., 85).

Central Park Ballad
Words and music by Charles Strouse.
Charles Strouse Music, 1985.
Introduced by Keith Corran and Ilene Kristen in the Off Broadway musical *Mayor* (85), based on New York City's Mayor Ed Koch.

The Chair
Words and music by Hank Cochran and Dean Dillon.
Tree Publishing Co., Inc., 1985/Larry Butler Music Co., 1985/
Blackwood Music Inc., 1985.
Best-selling record by George Strait from the album *Something Special*
(MCA, 85).

Cherish
Words and music by Ronald Bell, Charles Smith, Robert Bell, James
Taylor, George Brown, Curtis Williams, and James Bonneford.
Delightful Music Ltd., 1984.
Best-selling record by Kool & The Gang from the album *Emergency*
(De-Lite, 85).

Children's Crusade (English)
Words and music by Sting (pseudonym for Gordon Sumner).
Magnetic, England, 1985/Reggatta Music, Ltd., 1985/Illegal Songs,
Inc., 1985.
Introduced by Sting on the album *The Dream of the Blue Turtles* (A &
M, 85).

Closest Thing to Perfect
Words and music by Michael Omartian, Bruce Sudano, and Jermaine
Jackson.
Golden Torch Music Corp., 1985/See This House Music/Gold
Horizon Music Corp./Black Stallion/Soft Summer Songs.
Best-selling record by Jermaine Jackson from the album *Jermaine Jackson* (Arista, 85). Featured in the film *Perfect* (85).

Cool It Now
See *Popular Music, 1980-1984.*

Count Me Out
Words and music by Vincent Brantley and Rick Timas.
New Generation Music, 1985.
Best-selling record by New Edition from the album *All for Love* (MCA,
85).

Country Boy
Words and music by Tony Colton, Ray Smith, and Albert Lee.
Ackee Music Inc., 1977.
Best-selling record by Ricky Skaggs from the album *Country Boy* (Epic,
85).

Country Girls
Words and music by Troy Seals and Eddie Setser.
Warner-Tamerlane Publishing Corp., 1984/WB Music Corp., 1984/
Two-Sons Music, 1984.

33

Best-selling record by John Schneider from the album *Too Good to Stop Now* (MCA, 85).

The Cowboy Rides Away
Words and music by Sonny Throckmorton and Casey Kelly.
Cross Keys Publishing Co., Inc., 1984/Himownself's Music Co., 1984/Tight List Music Inc., 1984.
Best-selling record by George Strait from the album *Does Fort Worth Ever Cross Your Mind?* (MCA, 84).

Crazy
Words and music by Kenny Rogers and Richard Marx.
Lionsmate Music, 1984/Security Hogg Music, 1984.
Best-selling record by Kenny Rogers from the album *What About Me* (RCA, 85).

Crazy for You
Words by John Bettis, music by Jon Lind.
Warner-Tamerlane Publishing Corp., 1983/WB Music Corp./ Deertrack Music.
Best-selling record by Madonna (Warner Bros.). Introduced by Madonna in the film *Vision Quest*.

Crazy for Your Love
Words and music by James Pennington and Sonny LeMaire.
Careers Music Inc., 1984/Tree Publishing Co., Inc., 1984/Pacific Island Music, 1984.
Best-selling record by Exile from the album *Kentucky Hearts* (Epic, 85).

Crazy in the Night (Barking at Airplanes)
Words and music by Kim Carnes.
Moonwindow Music, 1985.
Best-selling record by Kim Carnes from the album *Barking at Airplanes* (EMI-America, 85).

Creatures of Love
Words and music by David Byrne.
Index Music, 1985/Bleu Disque Music.
Introduced by The Talking Heads on the album *Little Creatures* (Sire, 85).

Creepin'
Words and music by Stevie Wonder.
Jobete Music Co., Inc., 1985/Black Bull Music, 1985.
Performed by Luther Vandross in the album *The Night I Fell in Love* (Epic, 85).

Cry (English)
Words and music by Kevin Godley and Lol Creme.
Man-Ken Music Ltd., 1985.
Best-selling record by Godley and Creme from the album *The History Mix Volume I* (Polygram, 85).

Curves
Words and music by Preston Glass and Narada Michael Walden.
Bell Boy Music, 1985/Gratitude Sky Music, Inc., 1985.
Introduced by Siedah Garrett in the film *Vision Quest* (85).

D

Dancing in the Streets
Revived by Mick Jagger and David Bowie (EMI-America, 85). See *Popular Music, 1920-1979.* All proceeds from this 1985 recording were donated to fight famine in Africa and the United States.

Dare Me
Words and music by Sam Lorber and Dave Innis.
WB Music Corp., 1985/Bob Montgomery Music Inc., 1985/Dave Innis Music, 1985.
Best-selling record by The Pointer Sisters from the album *Contact* (RCA, 85).

Dark Eyes
Words and music by Bob Dylan.
Special Rider Music, 1985.
Introduced by Bob Dylan on the album *Empire Burlesque* (Columbia, 85).

Desperados Waiting for a Train
Words and music by Guy Clark.
Chappell & Co., Inc., 1973/World Song Publishing, Inc.
Revived by Waylon Jennings, Willie Nelson, Johnny Cash, and Kris Kristofferson on the album *Highwayman* (Columbia, 85). Nominated for a National Academy of Recording Arts and Sciences Award, Country Song of the Year, 1985.

Dixie Road
Words and music by Don Goodman, Mary Ann Kennedy, and Pam Rose.
Southern Soul Music, 1981/Window Music Publishing Inc.
Best-selling record by Lee Greenwood from the album *Streamline* (MCA, 85).

Don't Call Him a Cowboy
Words and music by Deborah Kay Hupp, Johnny McRae, and Brian Morrison.
Southern Nights Music Co., 1984.
Best-selling record by Conway Twitty from the album *Don't Call Him a Cowboy* (Warner Bros., 85).

Don't Call It Love
Words by Dean Pitchford, music by Tom Snow.
Pzazz Music, 1985/Snow Music, 1985.
Best-selling record by Dolly Parton from the album *Real Love* (RCA, 85).

Don't Come Around Here No More
Words and music by Tom Petty and Dave Stewart.
Gone Gator Music, 1985/Blue Network Music Inc.
Best-selling record by Tom Petty & The Heartbreakers from the album *Southern Accents* (MCA, 85).

Don't Forget Your Way Home
Words and music by Ed Hunnicutt and John Raymond Brannen.
Tapadero Music, 1985/Young Beau Music, 1985.
Introduced by Reba McIntire on the album *Have I Got a Deal for You* (MCA, 85).

Don't Lose My Number (English)
Words and music by Phil Collins.
Pun Music Inc., London, England, 1985.
Best-selling record by Phil Collins from the album *No Jacket Required* (Atlantic, 85).

Don't Run Wild
Words and music by Dan Zanes, Tom Lloyd, and James Ralston.
Big Thrilling Music, 1985/Of the Fire Music, 1985.
Introduced by The Del Fuegos on the album *Boston, Mass* (Slash, 85).

Don't Say No Tonight
Words and music by R. Broomfield and McKinley Horton.
Philly World Music Co., 1985.
Best-selling record by Eugene Wilde from the album *Serenade* (Philly World, 85).

Don't You (Forget About Me)
Words and music by Keith Forsey and Steve Schiff.
MCA, Inc., 1985/Music Corp. of America.
Best-selling record by Simple Minds (A & M, 85). Featured in the film *The Breakfast Club* (85).

Down on Love
Words and music by Mick Jones and Lou Gramm.
Somerset Songs Publishing, Inc., 1984/Evansongs Ltd., 1984/Stray
  Notes Music, 1984.
Best-selling record by Foreigner from the album *Agent Provocateur*
  (Atlantic, 85).

Down on the Farm
Words and music by John Greenebaum, Troy Seals, and Eddie
  Setser.
Make Believus Music, 1985/WB Music Corp., 1985/Two-Sons
  Music, 1985/Warner-Tamerlane Publishing Corp., 1985.
Introduced by Charley Pride (RCA, 85). Song about the plight of mod-
  ern day farmers presaged "Farm Aid" benefit concert to raise money
  for farmers several months later, whch starred Willie Nelson, Bob
  Dylan, and others.

Down to the Bone
Words and music by Dan Stuart and Steve Wynn.
Poisoned Brisket Music, 1985/Hang Dog Music, 1985.
Introduced by Danny and Dusty on the album *The Lost Weekend* (A
  & M, 85).

Dress You Up
Words and music by Peggy Stanziale and Andrea LaRusso.
House of Fun Music, 1984.
Best-selling record by Madonna in 1985 from the album *Like a Virgin*
  (Warner Bros., 84).

Drinkin' and Dreamin'
Words and music by Troy Seals and Max D. Barnes.
Two-Sons Music, 1985/Blue Lake Music/WB Music Corp.
Best-selling record by Waylon Jennings from the album *Turn the Page*
  (RCA, 85).

E

Easy Lover (English)
Words and music by Philip Bailey, Phil Collins, and Nathan East.
Pun Music Inc., London, England/Phil Collins, England/Sir & Trini
Music, 1984/New East Music.
Best-selling record by Philip Bailey with Phil Collins from the album
Chinese Wall (Columbia, 85).

Election Day (English)
Words and music by Nick Rhodes, Roger Taylor, and Simon LeBon.
Tritec Music Ltd., England, 1985.
Best-selling record by Arcadia from the album *So Red the Rose* (Capitol,
85).

Emergency
Words and music by George Brown, Ronald Bell, Charles Smith,
James Taylor, Robert Bell, Curtis Williams, and James Bonneford.
Delightful Music Ltd., 1984.
Best-selling record by Kool & The Gang from the album *Emergency*
(De-Lite, 85).

Every Time You Go Away
Words and music by Daryl Hall.
Unichappell Music Inc., 1980/Hot Cha Music Co., 1980.
Best-selling record by Paul Young from the album *The Secret of Associa-
tion* (Columbia, 85). Nominated for a National Academy of Record-
ing Arts and Sciences Award, Song of the Year, 1985.

Everybody Dance
Words and music by Jesse Johnson and Ta Mara.
Crazy People Music/Almo Music Corp., 1985/Almo Music Corp.,
1985.
Best-selling record by Ta Mara & The Seen from the album Ta Mara &
The Seen (A & M, 85).

Everybody Wants to Rule the World (English)
Words and music by Roy Orzabal, Ian Stanley, and Chris Hughes.
Amusements Ltd., England/Nymph Music, 1985.
Best-selling record by Tears for Fears from the album *Songs from the Big Chair* (Mercury, 85).

Everything I Need (Australian)
Words and music by Colin Hay.
April Music, Inc., 1985.
Introduced by Men at Work on the album *Two Hearts* (Columbia, 85).

Everything She Wants (English)
Words and music by George Michael.
Chappell & Co., Inc., 1984.
Best-selling record by Wham! in 1985 from the album *Make It Big* (Columbia, 84).

F

Face the Face (English)
Words and music by Pete Townshend.
Eel Pie Music, England, 1985.
Best-selling record by Pete Townshend from the album *White City*
(Atco, 85).

Fallin' in Love
Words and music by Randy Goodrum and Brent Maher.
April Music, Inc., 1985/Random Notes, 1985/Welbeck Music Corp.,
1985/Blue Quill Music, 1985.
Best-selling record by Sylvia from the album *One Step Closer* (RCA, 85).

Fish Below the Ice (English)
Words and music by Allen, Barry Andrews, Martin Barker, and
Marsh.
Point Music Ltd., England, 1985.
Introduced by Shriekback on the album *Oil and Gold* (Island, 85).

Flip Ya Flip
Words and music by Nils Lofgren.
Hilmer Music Publishing Co., 1985.
Introduced by Nils Lofgren on the album *Flip* (Columbia, 85).

Foolish Heart
Words and music by Steve Perry and Randy Goodrum.
Street Talk Tunes, 1984/April Music, Inc., 1984/Random Notes,
1984.
Best-selling record by Steve Perry in 1985 from the album *Street Talk*
(Columbia, 84).

Forever Man (English)
Words and music by Jerry Lynn Williams.
Blackwood Music Inc., 1985/Urge Music.
Best-selling record by Eric Clapton from the album *Behind the Sun*
(Warner Bros., 85).

Forgiving You Was Easy
Words and music by Willie Nelson.
Willie Nelson Music Inc., 1984.
Best-selling record by Willie Nelson from the album *Me and Paul* (Columbia, 85).

Fortress Around Your Heart (English)
Words and music by Sting (pseudonym for Gordon Sumner).
Reggatta Music, Ltd., 1985.
Best-selling record by Sting from the album *The Dream of the Blue Turtles* (A & M, 85).

40 Hour Week (for a Livin')
Words and music by Dave Loggins, Lisa Silver, and Don Schlitz.
Music Corp. of America, 1984/MCA, Inc./Leeds Music Corp./ Patchwork Music/Don Schlitz Music.
Best-selling record by Alabama from the album *40 Hour Week* (RCA, 85). Nominated for a National Academy of Recording Arts and Sciences Award, Country Song of the Year, 1985.

Four in the Morning (I Can't Take Anymore)
Words and music by Jack Blades.
Kid Bird Music, 1985.
Best-selling record by Night Ranger from the album *Seven Wishes* (MCA, 85).

Frankie (English)
Words and music by Joy Denny.
Atlantic Recording Corp., England, 1985.
Best-selling record by Sister Sledge from the album *When the Boys Meet the Girls* (Atlantic, 85).

Free Nelson Mandela (English)
Words and music by Jerry Dammers and Rhoda Dakar.
Plangent Visions Music, Inc., London, England, 1984.
Introduced by Special AKA (Chrysalis, 85). Re-released to capitalize on late 1985 anti-apartheid sentiments inspired by "Sun City." Mandela is one of South Africa's jailed Black leaders.

Freedom (English)
Words and music by George Michael.
Chappell & Co., Inc., 1984.
Best-selling record by Wham! in 1985 from the album *Make It Big* (Columbia, 84).

Freeway of Love
Words and music by Narada Michael Walden and Jeffrey Cohen.
Gratitude Sky Music, Inc., 1985/Polo Grounds Music.

Best-selling record by Aretha Franklin from the album *Who's Zoomin' Who* (Arista, 85). Won a National Academy of Recording Arts and Sciences Award, Rhythm 'n Blues Song of the Year, 1985.

Freeze Tag
Words and music by Suzanne Vega.
Waifersongs Ltd., 1985/AGF Music Ltd., 1985.
Introduced by Suzanne Vega on the album *Suzanne Vega* (A & M, 85).

Fresh
Words and music by James Taylor, Sandy Linzner, George Brown, Curtis Williams, Charles Smith, Ronald Bell, Robert Bell, and James Bonneford.
Delightful Music Ltd., 1984.
Best-selling record by Kool & The Gang from the album *Emergency* (De-Lite, 85).

Fright Night
Words and music by J. Lamont.
National League Music, 1985/Golden Torch Music Corp., 1985.
Introduced by J. Geils Band in the film *Fright Night* (85).

G

The Garden Path to Hell
Words and music by Rupert Holmes.
Holmes Line of Music, 1985.
Introduced by Cleo Laine in the musical *The Mystery of Edwin Drood*
(85), which moved to Broadway after originating at the Delacorte
Theatre in New York's Central Park.

Get It On (Bang a Gong) (English)
Revived by The Power Station on the album *The Power Station* (Capitol,
85). See *Popular Music, 1920-1979.*

Getcha Back
Words and music by Mike Love and Terry Melcher.
Careers Music Inc., 1985.
Best-selling record by The Beach Boys from the album *The Beach Boys*
(CBS, 85).

A Girls Night Out
Words and music by Jeff Hawthorne Bullock and Brent Maher.
Welbeck Music Corp., 1984/Blue Quill Music.
Best-selling record by The Judds from the album *Why Not Me* (RCA,
85).

Glory Days
Words and music by Bruce Springsteen.
Bruce Springsteen Publishing, 1984.
Best-selling record by Bruce Springsteen from the album *Born in the
U.S.A.* (Columbia, 84).

The Glow
Words and music by Willie Hutch.
Stone Diamond Music Corp., 1985.
Introduced by Willie Hutch in the film *The Last Dragon* (85).

Good Friends
Words and music by Joni Mitchell.
Crazy Crow Music, 1985.
Introduced by Joni Mitchell on the album *Dog Eat Dog* (Geffer, 85).

The Goonies 'R' Good Enough
Words and music by Cyndi Lauper, Stephen Lunt, and Arthur Stead.
Warner-Tamerlane Publishing Corp., 1985.
Best-selling record by Cyndi Lauper (Portrait, 85). Introduced in the
film *The Goonies* (85).

Gotta Get You Home Tonight
Words and music by McKinley Horton and Ronnie Broomfield.
Screen Gems-EMI Music Inc., 1984.
Best-selling record by Eugene Wilde from the album *Eugene Wilde*
(Atlantic, 85).

Gravity
Words and music by Michael Sembello.
WB Music Corp., 1985/Gravity Raincoat Music, 1985.
Introduced by Michael Sembello in the film *Cocoon* (85).

H

Hangin' on a String
Words and music by Carl McIntosh, Jane Eugene, and Steve Nichol.
Brampton Music Ltd., England/Virgin Music Ltd., 1985.
Best-selling record by Loose Ends from the album *A Little Spice* (MCA, 85).

Hanging on a Heartbeat
Words and music by Rob Hyman, Eric Bazilian, Glenn Goss, and Jeff Ziv.
Human Boy Music, 1982/Dub Notes, 1982.
Introduced by The Hooters on the album *Nervous Night* (Columbia, 85).

Have Mercy
Words and music by Paul Kennerley.
Irving Music Inc., 1985.
Best-selling record by The Judds from the album *Rockin' with Rhythm* (RCA/Curb, 85).

Heart of the Country
Words and music by Wendy Waldman and D Lowery.
Sheddhouse Music, 1985/Screen Gems-EMI Music Inc., 1984/Moon & Stars Music, 1985.
Best-selling record by Kathy Mattea from the album *From My Heart* (Mercury, 85).

The Heat Is On
Words by Keith Forsey, music by Harold Faltermeyer.
Famous Music Corp., 1985.
Best-selling record by Glenn Frey (MCA, 85). Introduced in the film *Beverly Hills Cop* (85); featured on its soundtrack album.

Heaven (Canadian)
Words and music by Bryan Adams and Jim Vallance.
Adams Communications, Inc., 1984/Irving Music Inc.

Introduced in the film *A Night in Heaven* (83). Best-selling record by Bryan Adams from the album *Reckless* (A & M, 85).

Hello Mary Lou
Revived by The Statler Brothers on the album *Pardners in Rhyme* (Mercury, 85). See *Popular Music, 1920-1979.*

Here I Am Again
Words and music by Shel Silverstein.
Evil Eye Music Inc., 1985.
Best-selling record by Johnny Rodriquez (Epic, 85).

Hero Takes a Fall
Words and music by Susanna Hoffs and Vicki Peterson.
Bangophile Music/Illegal Songs, Inc., 1984.
Introduced by The Bangles on the album *All Over the Place* (Columbia, 85).

High Horse
Words and music by James Ibbotson.
Unami Music, 1984.
Best-selling record by Nitty Gritty Dirt Band on the album *Partners, Brothers, and Friends* (Warner Bros.,85).

High on You
Words and music by Frankie Sullivan and Jim Peterik.
Rude Music, 1984/WB Music Corp./Easy Action Music.
Best-selling record by Survivor in 1985 from the album *Vital Signs* (Epic, 84).

High School Nights
Words and music by Dave Edmunds, Sam Gould, and John David.
John David Music Ltd., England/Mel-Bren Music Inc., 1985/Albion Music Ltd.
Introduced by Dave Edmunds in the film *Porky's Revenge* (85).

Highwayman
Words and music by Jim Webb.
White Oak Songs, 1977.
Introduced by Waylon Jennings, Willie Nelson, Johnny Cash, and Kris Kristofferson on the album *The Highwayman* (Columbia, 85). Won a National Academy of Recording Arts and Sciences Award, Country Song of the Year, 1985.

Honor Bound
Words and music by Charlie Black, Thomas Rocco, and Austin Roberts.
Chappell & Co., Inc., 1984/Bibo Music Publishers, 1984/MCA, Inc.,

1984/Chriswald Music, 1984/Hopi Sound Music, 1984.

Best-selling record by Earl Thomas Conley from the album *Treadin'
Water* (RCA, 85).

How Old Are You

Words and music by Loudon Wainwright.

Snowden Music, 1983.

Introduced by Loudon Wainwright on the album *I'm All Right* (Columbia, 85), Wainwright's biting reply to critics who wonder whatever
became of him and how he squandered his talent.

How Soon Is Now (English)

Words by Tommy Morrissey, music by Johnny Marr.

Morrissey/Marr Songs Ltd., England, 1985.

Introduced by The Smiths on the album *Meat Is Murder* (Sire, 85).

How'm I Doin'

Words and music by Charles Strouse.

Charles Strouse Music, 1985.

Introduced by Lenny Wolpe in the off Broadway musical *Mayor* (85).
The title is a favorite question from New York City Mayor Edward
I. Koch, whose administration was the basis of this play.

I

I Ain't Got Nobody
Words and music by Roger Graham and Spencer Williams.
Chappell & Co., Inc., 1915, 1943/Intersong, USA Inc./Edwin H.
Morris Co./Jerry Vogel Music Co., Inc.
Revived by David Lee Roth as part of a medley with "Just a Gigolo,"
from the album *Crazy from the Heat* (Warner Bros., 85).

I Can't Hold Back
See *Popular Music, 1980-1984.*

I Don't Know Why You Don't Want Me
Words and music by Rosanne Cash and Rodney Crowell.
Chelcait Music, 1985/Atlantic Music Corp., 1985/Coolwell Music,
1985/Granite Music Corp., 1985.
Best-selling record by Rosanne Cash from the album *Rhythm and Ro-
mance* (Columbia, 85). Nominated for a National Academy of
Recording Arts and Sciences Award, Country Song of the Year, 1985.

I Don't Mind the Thorns (If You're the Rose)
Words and music by Jan Buckingham and Linda Young.
Warner-Tamerlane Publishing Corp., 1985/Pullman Music, 1985/
Duck Songs, 1985.
Best-selling record by Lee Greenwood from the album *Streamline*
(MCA, 85).

I Don't Think I'm Ready for You
Words and music by Stephen Dorff, Milton Brown, Burt Reynolds,
and Snuff Garrett.
Music Corp. of America, 1985/Happy Trails.
Introduced by by Anne Murray in the film *Stick* (85).

I Don't Want to Do It
Words and music by Bob Dylan.
Special Rider Music, 1985.
Introduced by George Harrison in the film *Porky's Revenge* (85).

I Drink Alone
Words and music by George Thorogood.
Del Sound Music, 1985.
Introduced by George Thorogood on the album *Maverick* (EMI-America, 85).

I Feel for You
See *Popular Music, 1980-1984.* Nominated for a National Academy of Recording Arts and Sciences Award, Rhythm 'n Blues Song of the Year, 1985.

I Fell in Love Again Last Night
Words and music by Paul Overstreet and Thomas Schuyler.
Writer's Group Music, 1985/Scarlet Moon Music, 1985.
Best-selling record by The Forester Sisters from the album *The Forester Sisters* (Warner Bros., 85).

I Have Never Felt This Way Before (English)
Words by Don Black, music by Andrew Lloyd Webber.
Dick James Music Inc., 1985.
Introduced by Bernadette Peters in the musical *Song and Dance* (85).

I Knew Him So Well (English)
Words by Tim Rice, words and music by Bjorn Ulvaeus and Benny Andersson.
Union Songs Musikfoerlag, Sweden/MCA, Inc., 1985.
Introduced by Elaine Paige on the album *Chess* (RCA, 85) for the musical which is scheduled to open in England in 1986.

I Know the Way to You by Heart
Words and music by Tony Laiola.
Blue Lake Music, 1983.
Best-selling record by Vern Gosdin from the album *Time Stood Still* (Compleat, 85). Introduced by Marlow Tackett.

I Miss You
Words and music by Lynn Malsby.
Spectrum VII, 1985.
Best-selling record by Klymaxx from the album *Meeting in the Ladies Room* (MCA/Constellation, 85).

I Need More of You
Words and music by David Bellamy.
Bellamy Brothers Music, 1985/Famous Music Corp., 1985.
Best-selling record by The Bellamy Brothers from the album *Howard and David* (MCA, 85).

I Saw It on TV
Words and music by John Fogerty.
Wenaha Music Co., 1984.
Introduced by John Fogerty on the album *Centerfield* (Warner Bros., 85).

I Sweat (Going Through the Motions)
Words and music by Nona Hendryx.
Eat Your Heart Out Music, 1984.
Introduced by Nona Hendryx in the film *Perfect* (85).

I Told a Lie to My Heart
Words and music by Hank Williams.
Acuff-Rose Publications Inc., 1984.
Introduced by Willie Nelson on the album *Half Nelson* (Columbia, 85).
    This is a previously unreleased demo.

I Want to Know What Love Is
Words and music by Mick Jones.
Somerset Songs Publishing, Inc., 1984/Evansongs Ltd.
Best-selling record by Foreigner from the album *Agent Provocateur* (Atlantic, 85). Nominated for a National Academy of Recording Arts and Sciences Award, Song of the Year, 1985.

I Wish He Didn't Trust Me So Much
Words and music by P. LuBoff, Harold Payne, and J. Eubanks.
Pea Pod Music, 1985/Pass It On Music, 1985/Legs Music, Inc., 1985.
Best-selling record by Bobby Womack from the album *So Many Rivers* (MCA, 85).

I Wonder If I Take You Home
Words and music by Full Force.
My My Music, 1985/Mokajumbi, 1985/Personal Music, 1985.
Best-selling record by Lisa Lisa/Cult Jam with Full Force from the album *Lisa Lisa/Cult Jam with Full Force* (Columbia, 85).

I Would Die 4 U
Words and music by Prince Rogers Nelson.
Controversy Music, 1984/WB Music Corp.
Best-selling record by Prince & The Revolution in 1985 from the album *Purple Rain* (Warner Bros., 84). Featured in the film *Purple Rain* (84).

If I Had a Rocket Launcher (Canadian)
Words and music by Bruce Cockburn.
Golden Mountain Music Inc., 1984.
Best-selling record by Bruce Cockburn in 1985 from the album *Stealing Fire* (Gold Mountain, 84).

If I Loved You
Revived by Barbra Streisand on *The Broadway Album* (Columbia, 85). See *Popular Music, 1920-1979.*

If You Love Somebody Set Them Free (English)
Words and music by Sting (pseudonym for Gordon Sumner). Reggatta Music, Ltd., 1985.
Best-selling record by Sting from the album *The Dream of the Blue Turtles* (A & M, 85).

I'll Keep It with Mine
Released by Bob Dylan on the five-record retrospective *Biograph* (Columbia, 85). Previously recorded by Nico with the Velvet Underground and by others. See *Popular Music, 1920-1979.*

I'll Never Stop Loving You
Words and music by Dave Loggins and J. D. Martin.
Music Corp. of America, 1985/Leeds Music Corp., 1985/Patchwork Music, 1985.
Best-selling record by Gary Morris from the album *Anything Goes* (Warner Bros., 85).

(No Matter How High I Get) I'll Still Be Lookin' Up to You
Words and music by Bobby Womack and P. Kisch.
ABKCO Music Inc., 1985/Ashtray Music.
Best-selling record by Wilton Felder featuring Bobby Womack, from the album *Secrets* (MCA, 85).

I'm for Love
Words and music by Hank Williams, Jr.
Bocephus Music Inc., 1985.
Best-selling record by Hank Williams, Jr. from the album *Five-O* (Warner Bros., 85).

I'm Goin' Down
Words and music by Bruce Springsteen.
Bruce Springsteen Publishing, 1984.
Best-selling record by Bruce Springsteen in 1985 from the album *Born in the U.S.A.* (Columbia, 84).

I'm Gonna Tear Your Playhouse Down
Best-selling record by Paul Young from the album *The Secret of Association* (Columbia, 85). See *Popular Music, 1920-1979.*

I'm on Fire
Words and music by Bruce Springsteen.
Bruce Springsteen Publishing, 1984.

Best-selling record by Bruce Springsteen in 1985 from the album *Born in the U.S.A.* (Columbia, 84).

I'm Your Man (English)
Words and music by George Michael.
Chappell & Co., Inc., 1985.
Best-selling record by Wham! (Columbia, 85).

Impossible Dreamer
Words and music by Joni Mitchell.
Crazy Crow Music, 1985.
Introduced by Joni Mitchell on the album *Dog Eat Dog* (Geffen, 85).

In a New York Minute
Words and music by Michael Garvin, Chris Waters, and Tom Shapiro.
Tree Publishing Co., Inc., 1985/O'Lyric Music, 1985.
Best-selling record by Ronnie McDowell from the album *In a New York Minute* (Epic, 85).

In Buddy's Eyes
Words and music by Stephen Sondheim.
Herald Square Music Co.
Revived by Barbara Cook on the album *Follies* (RCA, 85). This concert album featured the original cast of the 1971 musical.

In Love with the Flame (English)
Words and music by Linda Thompson and Betsy Cook.
Firesign Music Ltd., England, 1985/Chappell & Co., Inc., 1985.
Introduced by Linda Thompson on the album *One Clear Moment* (Warner Bros., 85).

In My House
Words and music by Rick James.
Stone City Music, 1985.
Best-selling record by The Mary Jane Girls from the album *Only Four You* (Motown, 85).

Invincible (Theme from *The Legend of Billie Jean*)
Words and music by Holly Knight and Simon Climie.
Makiki Publishing Co., Ltd., 1985/Arista Music, Inc., 1985/Rare Blue Music, Inc., 1985.
Best-selling record by Pat Benatar (Chrysalis, 85). Introduced in the film *The Legend of Billie Jean*.

Itchin' for a Scratch
Words and music by Robin Halpin, Steve Stein, Douglas Wimbish, and Keith LeBlanc, words and music by Force M.D.'s.

Atlantic Recording Corp., England, 1985/Tee Girl Music, 1985/Tee Boy Music, 1985.

Introduced by Force M.D.'s (T-Boy, 85). Featured in the film *Rappin'* (85).

It's Only Love (Canadian)

Words and music by Bryan Adams and Jim Valance.

Adams Communications, Inc., 1985/Calypso Toonz, 1985/Irving Music Inc., 1985.

Best-selling record by Bryan Adams and Tina Turner from the album *Reckless* (A & M, 85).

J,K

Jamie
Words and music by Ray Parker, Jr.
Raydiola Music, 1984.
Best-selling record by Ray Parker, Jr. from the album *Chartbusters* (Arista, 85).

Jesse (English)
Words and music by China Burton.
Virgin Music Ltd., 1984.
Introduced by Julian Lennon on the album *Valotte* (Atlantic, 84).

Jungle Fever
Words by Michael Colby, music by Paul Katz.
No publisher available, 1985.
Introduced by Elizabeth Austin in the musical *Tales of Tinseltown* (85).

Jungle Love
Words and music by Jesse Johnson, Morris Day, and Prince Rogers Nelson.
Tionna Music, 1984/WB Music Corp., 1984.
Best-selling record by The Time from the album *Ice Cream Castle* (Warner Bros., 85). Performed by Morris Day and The Time in the film *Purple Rain*.

Just a Gigolo
Revived by David Lee Roth in a medley with "I Ain't Got Nobody" from the album *Crazy from the Heat* (Warner Bros., 85). See *Popular Music, 1920-1979*.

Just Another Night (English)
Words and music by Mick Jagger.
Promopub B. V., Netherlands, 1985.
Best-selling record by Mick Jagger from the album *She's the Boss* (Columbia, 85).

Just As I Am
Words and music by Dick Wagner and Robert Hegel.
Don Kirshner Music Inc., 1982/Rightsong Music Inc./Mystery Man
    Music.
Best-selling record by Air Supply from the album *Air Supply* (Arista,
    85).

Just One of the Guys
Words and music by Marc Tanner and Jon Reede.
Golden Torch Music Corp., 1985/JonoSongs, 1985/Otherwise
    Publishing.
Introduced by Shalamar in the film *Just One of the Guys* (85).

Kayleigh (English)
Words and music by Fish (pseudonym for Derek William Dick).
Charisma Music Publishing Co., Ltd., England, 1985/Chappell &
    Co., Inc., 1985.
Best-selling record by Marillion from the album *Misplaced Childhood*
    (Capitol, 85).

Keep It Confidential
Words and music by Ellie Greenwich, Jeffrey Kent, and Ellen Foley.
Jent Music Inc., 1985/My Own Music/Urban Noise Music.
Introduced by Gina Taylor in the Broadway musical *Leader of the Pack*
    (85).

Keeping the Faith
Words and music by Billy Joel.
Joelsongs, 1983.
Best-selling record by Billy Joel in 1985 from the album *An Innocent
    Man* (Columbia, 84).

Knight Moves
Words and music by Suzanne Vega.
Waifersongs Ltd., 1985/AGF Music Ltd., 1985.
Introduced by Suzanne Vega on the album *Suzanne Vega* (A & M, 85).

Knocking at Your Back Door
Words and music by Ritchie Blackmore, Roger Glover, and Ian
    Gillan.
Blackmore Music Ltd., 1985/Rugged Music Ltd., 1985/Pussy Music
    Ltd., 1985.
Best-selling record by Deep Purple in 1985 from the album *Perfect
    Stranger* (Mercury, 84).

L

Ladder of Success (English)
Words and music by Ray Davies.
Davray Music, Ltd., London, England, 1985.
Introduced by Ray Davies in the film *Return to Waterloo* (85), which
  he wrote and starred in.

The Ladies Who Lunch
Revived by Barbra Streisand on *The Broadway Album* (Columbia, 85).
  See *Popular Music, 1920-1979.*

A Lady Like You
Words and music by Jim Weatherly and Keith Stegall.
Blackwood Music Inc., 1984/Bright Sky Music, 1984/Charlie Monk
  Music, 1984.
Best-selling record by Glen Campbell from the album *Letter to Home*
  (Atlantic, 85).

Land of 1000 Dances
Revived by Wrestlers (Epic, 85). Epitomizing rock 'n' wrestling mania,
  which probably began with Freddie Blassie and "Hey, Ya Pencil-Neck
  Geek" from the late seventies, this remake featured a brigade of profes-
  sional wrestlers of the eighties, including Roddy Piper, Junkyard Dog,
  Mean Gene Okerlund, and Captain Lou Albano. See *Popular
  Music, 1920-1979.*

Lasso the Moon
Words and music by Steven Dorff and Milton Brown.
Ensign Music Corp., 1985.
Introduced by Gary Morris in the film *Rustler's Rhapsody* (85).

The Last Dragon
Words and music by Norman Whitfield and B. Miller.
Stone Diamond Music Corp., 1985/Golden Torch Music Corp.,
  1985.
Introduced by Dwight David in the film *The Last Dragon* (85).

Lay Down Your Weary Tune
A Bob Dylan classic recorded in 1963 and re-released by Dylan on the
five-record retrospective *Biograph* (Columbia, 85). See *Popular
Music, 1920-1979.*

Lay Your Hands on Me (English)
Words and music by Tom Bailey, Alannah Currie, and Joe Leeway.
Zomba Enterprises, Inc., 1985.
Best-selling record by Thompson Twins from the album *Here's to Future
Days* (Arista, 85). Introduced in the film *Perfect* (85).

Let Him Go
Words and music by William Wadhams.
Famous Music Corp., 1984/Big Wad/Famous Music Corp., 1984.
Best-selling record by Animotion from the album *Animotion* (Mercury,
85).

Let Me Dance for You
Words by Edward Kleban, music by Marvin Hamlisch.
Wren Music Co., Inc., 1985/American Compass Music Corp., 1985.
Introduced in the film version of the hit musical *A Chorus Line* (85).

Let Me Down Easy (English)
Words and music by Bryan Adams and Jim Vallance.
Irving Music Inc., 1985/Adams Communications, Inc., 1985/Calypso
Toonz, 1985.
Introduced by Roger Daltrey on the album *Under a Raging Moon*
(Atlantic, 85).

Lie to You for Your Love
Words and music by Frankie Miller, David Bellamy, Howard
Bellamy, and Jeff Barry.
Rare Blue Music, Inc., 1985/Bellamy Brothers Music, 1985/Steeple
Chase Music, 1985.
Best-selling record by The Bellamy Brothers from the album *Howard
and David* (MCA, 85).

Life in One Day (English)
Words and music by Howard Jones.
Warner-Tamerlane Publishing Corp., 1985.
Best-selling record by Howard Jones from the album *Life in One Day*
(Elektra, 85).

Lights of Downtown
Words and music by Stephen McCarthy.
Huevos Rancheros Music, 1985.
Introduced by The Long Ryders on the album *State of Our Union*
(Island, 85).

Like a Virgin
Words and music by Billy Steinberg and Tom Kelly.
Billy Steinberg Music, 1984/Denise Barry Music.
Best-selling record by Madonna in 1985 from the album *Like a Virgin* (Warner Bros., 84).

Little Things, see **Baby, It's the Little Things.**

Little Wild One (No. 5)
Words and music by Marshall Crenshaw.
Colgems-EMI Music Inc., 1985/House of Greed Music, 1985.
Introduced by Marshall Crenshaw on the album *Downtown* (Warner Bros., 85).

Lonely Ol' Night
Words and music by John Cougar Mellencamp.
Riva Music Ltd., 1985.
Best-selling record by John Cougar Mellencamp from the album *Scarecrow* (Mercury, 85).

Lost in the Fifties Tonight (In the Still of the Night)
Words and music by Mike Reid, Troy Seals, and Freddy Parris.
Lodge Hall Music, Inc., 1985/WB Music Corp./Llee Corp.
Best-selling record by Ronnie Milsap from *Greatest Hits, Vol. 2* (RCA, 85). The central musical theme is from one of rock 'n' roll's greatest "do-wop" classics. Nominated for a National Academy of Recording Arts and Sciences Award, Country Song of the Year, 1985.

A Love Bizarre
Words and music by Sheila Escovedo and Prince Rogers Nelson.
Sister Fate Music, 1985/Controversy Music, 1985.
Best-selling record by Sheila E. from the album *Romance 1600* (Warner Bros., 85).

Love Don't Care (Whose Heart It Breaks)
Words and music by Earl Thomas Conley and Randy Scruggs.
Labor of Love Music, 1984/April Music, Inc./Blackwood Music Inc.
Best-selling record by Earl Thomas Conley from the album *Treadin' Water* (RCA, 85).

Love Is Alive
Words and music by Kent Robbins.
Irving Music Inc., 1984.
Best-selling record by The Judds from the album *Why Not Me* (RCA, 85). Nominated for a National Academy of Recording Arts and Sciences Award, Country Song of the Year, 1985.

Love Is the Seventh Wave (English)
Words and music by Sting (pseudonym for Gordon Sumner).
Magnetic, England, 1985/Reggatta Music, Ltd./Illegal Songs, Inc.
Best-selling record by Sting from the album *The Dream of the Blue Turtles* (A & M, 85).

Love Light in Flight
Words and music by Stevie Wonder.
Jobete Music Co., Inc., 1984/Black Bull Music, 1984.
Best-selling record by Stevie Wonder from the album *The Woman in Red* (Motown, 85). Introduced in the film *The Woman in Red* (85).

Love Radiates Around
Words and music by Mark Johnson.
Cold Weather Music, 1980/New Media Music.
Introduced by The Roches on the album *Another World* (Warner Bros., 85).

Love Theme from *St. Elmo's Fire* (Instrumental)
Words and music by David Foster.
Gold Horizon Music Corp., 1985/Foster Frees Music Inc., 1985.
Best-selling record by David Foster (Atlantic, 85). Introduced in the film *St. Elmo's Fire* (85).

Love to See You
Words and music by Suzzy Roche.
Deshufflin' Inc., 1985.
Introduced by The Roches on the album *Another World* (Warner Bros., 85).

Lover Boy
Words and music by Keith Diamond, Billy Ocean, and Robert John Lange.
Zomba Enterprises, Inc., 1984/Willesden Music, Inc., 1984.
Best-selling record by Billy Ocean in 1985 from the album *Suddenly* (Arista, 84).

Lovergirl
Words and music by Teena Marie (pseudonym for Teena Marie Brockert).
CBS Inc., 1984/Midnight Magnet, 1985.
Best-selling record by Teena Marie from the album *Starchild* (Epic, 85).

Love's Calling
Words and music by Sam Cooke.
ABKCO Music Inc., 1984.
Introduced by Womack and Womack on the album *Radio M.U.S.C. Man* (Elektra, 85). Linda Womack is the daughter of the late Sam

Cooke. This song is one of twenty Cooke had been working on at the time of his death.

Lucky Girl
Words and music by Joni Mitchell.
Crazy Crow Music, 1985.
Introduced by Joni Mitchell on the album *Dog Eat Dog* (Geffen, 85).

M

Make My Life with You
Words and music by Gary Burr.
Garwin Music Inc., 1984/Sweet Karol Music, 1984.
Best-selling record by The Oak Ridge Boys from the album *Step on Out* (MCA, 85).

March of the Yuppies
Words and music by Charles Strouse.
Charles Strouse Music, 1985.
Introduced by Nancy Giles in the Off Broadway musical *Mayor* (85).

Marlene on the Wall
Words and music by Suzanne Vega.
Waifersongs Ltd., 1985/AGF Music Ltd., 1985.
Introduced by Suzanne Vega on the album *Suzanne Vega* (A & M, 85).
   This song is dedicated to Marlene Dietrich.

Material Girl
Words and music by Peter Brown and Robert Rans.
Minong Music, 1984.
Best-selling record by Madonna in 1985 from the album *Like a Virgin* (Warner Bros., 84).

Maureen, Maureen
Words and music by John Prine.
Big Ears Music Inc., 1985/Bruised Oranges, 1985.
Introduced by John Prine on the album *Aimless Love* (Oh Boy, 85).

Meat Is Murder (English)
Words by Tommy Morrissey, music by Johnny Marr.
Morrissey/Marr Songs Ltd., England, 1985.
Introduced by The Smiths on the album *Meat Is Murder* (Sire, 85).

Meet Me in Montana
Words and music by Paul Davis.

Web 4 Music Inc., 1984.
Best-selling record by Marie Osmond with Dan Seals from the album *There's No Stopping Your Heart* (Capitol, 85).

The Men All Pause
Words and music by Bernadette Cooper, Joyce Simmons, and D McDaniels.
Spectrum VII, 1984.
Best-selling record by Klymaxx from the album *Meeting in the Ladies Room* (MCA, 85). Featured in the film *The Slugger's Wife* (85).

Men Without Shame
Words and music by Slim Jim Phantom (pseudonym for James McDonnell), Lee Rocker, and Earl Slick (pseudonym for Frank Madeloni).
Pressed Ham Hits, 1985/Willesden Music, Inc., 1985/Oil Slick Music, 1985.
Best-selling record by Phantom, Rocker & Slick from the album *Phantom, Rocker & Slick* (EMI-America, 85).

Method of Modern Love
Words and music by Daryl Hall and Janna Allen.
Hot Cha Music Co., 1984/Unichappell Music Inc./Fust Buzza Music, Inc.
Best-selling record by Daryl Hall and John Oates in 1985 from the album *Big Bam Boom* (RCA, 84).

Miami Vice Theme
Words and music by Jan Hammer.
MCA, Inc., 1985.
Best-selling record by Jan Hammer (MCA, 85). Introduced on the television series *Miami Vice* (84).

Miracle Mile
Words and music by Dan Stuart and Steve Wynn.
Poisoned Brisket Music, 1985/Hang Dog Music, 1985.
Introduced by Danny and Dusty on the album *The Lost Weekend* (A & M, 85).

Misled
Words and music by Ronald Bell, James Taylor, Charles Smith, George Brown, Robert Bell, Curtis Williams, and James Bonneford.
Delightful Music Ltd., 1984.
Best-selling record by Kool & The Gang from the album *Emergency* (De-Lite, 85).

Miss Celie's Blues (Sisters)
Words and music by Quincy Jones and Rod Temperton, words by
Lionel Richie.
WB Music Corp., 1985/Rodsongs/Brockman Music.
Introduced by Tata Vega in the film *The Color Purple* (85). Nominated
for an Academy Award, Song of the Year, 1985.

Missing You
Words and music by Lionel Richie.
Brockman Enterprises Inc., 1984.
Best-selling record by Diana Ross in 1985 from the album *Swept Away*
(RCA, 84). This song is dedicated to Marvin Gaye, who was killed in
1984.

Mr. Telephone Man
Words and music by Ray Parker, Jr.
Raydiola Music, 1983.
Best-selling record by New Edition in 1985 from the album *New Edition*
(MCA, 84).

Modern Day Romance
Words and music by Kix Brooks (pseudonym for Leon Brooks) and
Daniel Tyler.
Golden Bridge Music, 1985/Mota Music, 1985/Oil Slick Music,
1985.
Best-selling record by Nitty Gritty Dirt Band from the album *Partners,
Brothers, and Friends* (Warner Bros., 85).

? (Modern Industry)
Words and music by David Kahne and Kendall Jones.
Bouillabaisse Music, England, 1985/Seesquared Music, 1985.
Introduced by Fishbone on the album *Fishbone* (Columbia, 85).

Money for Nothing (English)
Words and music by Mark Knopfler and Sting (pseudonym for
Gordon Sunmer).
Chariscourt Ltd., 1985/Almo Music Corp., 1985/Virgin Music Ltd.,
1985.
Best-selling record by Dire Straits from the album *Brothers in Arms*
(Warner Bros., 85). Nominated for National Academy of Recording
Arts and Sciences Awards, Record of the Year, 1985, and Song of the
Year, 1985.

Moonfall
Words and music by Rupert Holmes.
Holmes Line of Music, 1985.
Introduced by Howard McGillin in the musical *The Mystery of Edwin
Drood* (85).

Morning Desire
Words and music by Dave Loggins.
Leeds Music Corp., 1985/Patchwork Music, 1985.
Best-selling record by Kenny Rogers from the album *The Heart of the Matter* (RCA, 85).

Mrs. Green
Words and music by Michael Quercio.
Latin Songs, 1985.
Introduced by The Three O'Clock on the album *Arrive Without Travelling* (I.R.S., 85).

Muddy Water
Words and music by Roger Miller.
Roger Miller Music, 1985/Tree Publishing Co., Inc., 1985.
Introduced by Daniel Jenkins and Ron Richardson in the musical *Big River* (85).

Murphy's Romance
Words and music by Carole King.
Elorac Music, 1985.
Introduced by Carole King in the film *Murphy's Romance* (85).

My Baby's Got Good Timing
Words and music by Dan Seals and Bob McDill.
Pink Pig Music, 1984/Hall-Clement Publications, 1984.
Best-selling record by Dan Seals from the album *San Antone* (EMI-America, 85).

My Elusive Dreams
Revived by David Allan Coe on the album *Darlin' Darlin'* (Columbia, 85). See *Popular Music, 1920-1979.*

My Girl
Revived by Daryl Hall and John Oates (RCA, 85) as part of a medley with "The Way You Do the Things You Do." See *Popular Music, 1920-1979.*

My Mind Is on You
Words and music by Dave Loggins and Don Schlitz.
Leeds Music Corp., 1985/MCA, Inc., 1985/Patchwork Music, 1985/ Don Schlitz Music, 1985.
Introduced by Gus Hardin on the album *Wall of Tears* (RCA, 85).

My Only Love
Words and music by Jimmy Fortune.
Statler Brothers Music, 1984.

Best-selling record by The Statler Brothers from the album *Pardners in Rhyme* (Mercury, 85).

My Toot Toot, also known as **My Tu Tu**
Words and music by Sidney Simien.
Sid Sim Publishing, 1984/Flat Town Music.
Introduced by Rockin' Sidney on the album *My Zydeco Shoes Got the Zydeco Blues* (Maison de Soul). Best-selling record by Jean Knight (Malaco, 85) and Denise La Salle (Malaco, 85). This contagious Cajun item emanated from Louisiana and was one of the rare throwbacks to an earlier era when independent songs were covered by major labels.

My Tu Tu, see **My Toot Toot.**

Mystery Lady
Words and music by Keith Diamond, Billy Ocean, and James Woodley.
Zomba Enterprises, Inc., 1984/Willesden Music, Inc.
Introduced by Billy Ocean on the album *Suddenly* (Arista, 84).

N

Name of the Game
Words and music by Dan Hartman and Charlie Midnight.
Blackwood Music Inc., 1985.
Introduced by Dan Hartman in the film *Fletch* (85).

Natural High
Words and music by Freddy Powers.
Mount Shasta Music Inc., 1984.
Best-selling record by Merle Haggard from the album *Kern River* (Epic,
   85).

Neutron Dance
Words and music by Allee Willis and David Sembello.
Off Backstreet Music, 1985/Unicity Music, Inc., 1985.
Best-selling record by the Pointer Sisters in 1985 from the album *Break
   Out* (Planet, 84). Introduced in the film *Beverly Hills Cop* (85); in-
   cluded on the soundtrack album of the film.

Never
Words and music by Holly Knight, Walter Bloch, and Ann (Dustin)
   Wilson.
Makiki Publishing Co., Ltd., 1985/Arista Music, Inc., 1985/Strange
   Euphoria Music, 1985/Know Music, 1985.
Best-selling record by Heart from the album *Heart* (Capitol, 85).

Never Ending Story
Words and music by Giorgio Moroder and Keith Forsey.
Giorgio Moroder Publishing Co., 1984/Colgems-EMI Music Inc.,
   1984.
Best-selling record by Limahl from the album *Don't Suppose* (EMI-
   America, 85). Introduced in the film *Never Ending Story* (85).

Never Surrender (Canadian)
Words and music by Corey Hart.
Liesse Publishing, 1985.

Best-selling record by Corey Hart from the album *Boy in the Box* (EMI-America, 85).

New Attitude
Words and music by Sharon Robinson, Jonathan Gilutin, and Bunny Hull.
Unicity Music, Inc., 1985/Off Backstreet Music, 1985/Rockomatic Music, 1985/Brassheart Music, 1985/Robin Hill Music, 1985.
Best-selling record by Patti LaBelle from the album *Patti* (MCA, 85).
Nominated for a National Academy of Recording Arts and Sciences Award, Song of the Year, 1985.

New Looks
Words and music by Charles Fox.
WB Music Corp., 1985.
Introduced by Dr. John in the film *European Vacation* (85).

The Night Spanish Eddie Cashed It In, also known as **Spanish Eddie**
Words and music by David Palmer and Chuck Cochran.
Tyrell-Mann Music Corp., 1985/Glory Music Co., 1985.
Best-selling record by Laura Branigan from the album *Hold Me* (Atlantic, 85).

Nightshift
Words and music by Walter Orange, Dennis Lambert, and Frannie Golde.
Rightsong Music Inc., 1984/Franne Golde Music Inc., 1984/Tuneworks Music, 1984/Walter Orange Music, 1984.
Best-selling record by The Commodores from the album *Nightshift* (Motown, 85). This song is a tribute to Jackie Wilson and Marvin Gaye, who died in 1984, and is reminiscent in feel to the classic "Abraham, Martin, and John" Nominated for a National Academy of Recording Arts and Sciences Award, Song of the Year, 1985.

19 (English)
Words and music by Paul Hardcastle, W. Coutourie, and J. McCord.
Crysallis Records Inc., England, 1985/Virgin Music, Inc., 1985/Oval Music Co., 1985.
Best-selling record by Paul Hardcastle from the album *Rain Forest* (Chrysallis, 85). This is a musical soundtrack to a spoken vocal from the television docudrama *Vietnam Requiem* (85).

No More Lonely Nights
See *Popular Music, 1980-1984.*

Nobody Falls Like a Fool
Words and music by Peter McCann and M. Wright.

April Music, Inc., 1985/New & Used Music, 1985/Blackwood Music Inc., 1985/Land of Music Publishing, 1985.

Best-selling record by Earl Thomas Conley from *Greatest Hits* (RCA, 85).

Nobody Wants to Be Alone

Words and music by Michael Masser and Rhonda Fleming.

Almo Music Corp., 1985/Prince Street Music, 1985/Irving Music Inc., 1985/Eaglewood Music, 1985.

Best-selling record by Crystal Gayle from the album *Nobody Wants to Be Alone* (Warner Bros., 85).

Not Enough Love in the World

Words and music by Don Henley, Danny Kortchmar, and Ben Tench.

Cass County Music Co., 1984/Kortchmar Music.

Best-selling record by Don Henley (Warner Bros., 85). Probably among the most caustic lyrics of the year.

O

The Oak Tree
Words and music by Morris Day.
Ya D Sir Music, 1985.
Best-selling record by Morris Day from the album *The Color of Success* (Warner Bros., 85).

Obsession
Words and music by Holly Knight and Michael Desbarres.
Pacific Island Music, 1983/Careers Music Inc., 1983/Makiki Publishing Co., Ltd., 1983/Arista Music, Inc., 1983.
Best-selling record by Animotion from the album *Animotion* (Mercury, 85).

Oh, Sheila
Words and music by Mel Riley, Gordon Strozier, and Gerald Valentine.
Ready for the World Music, 1985/Excalibur Lace Music, 1985/ Trixie Lou Music, 1985/MCA, Inc., 1985/Off Backstreet Music, 1985/Walk on Moon Music, 1985.
Best-selling record by Ready for the World from the album *Ready for the World* (MCA, 85).

Old Hippie
Words and music by David Bellamy.
Bellamy Brothers Music, 1985.
Best-selling record by The Bellamy Brothers from the album *Howard and David* (MCA, 85).

The Old Man Down the Road
Words and music by John Fogerty.
Wenaha Music Co., 1984.
Best-selling record by John Fogerty from the album *Centerfield* (Warner Bros., 85).

Once Bitten
Words and music by Billy Steinberg, Tom Kelly, Michael Greeley, David Currier, and Linda Chase.
Billy Steinberg Music, 1985/Denise Barry Music, 1985/Polifer Music, 1985/Brigitte Baby Publishing, 1985.
Introduced by 3 Speed in the film *Once Bitten* (85).

One Clear Moment
Words and music by Linda Thompson and Betsy Cook.
Firesign Music Ltd., England, 1984/Chappell & Co., Inc., 1984.
Introduced by Linda Thompson on the album *One Clear Moment* (Warner Bros., 85).

One Lonely Night
Words and music by Neal Doughty.
Jonisongs, 1984.
Best-selling record by REO Speedwagon from the album *Wheels Are Turning* (Epic, 85).

One More Night (English)
Words and music by Phil Collins.
Pun Music Inc., London, England, 1984.
Best-selling record by Phil Collins from the album *No Jacket Required* (Atlantic, 85).

One Night in Bangkok (English-Swedish)
English words and music by Benny Andersson, Tim Rice, and Bjorn Ulvaeus.
Union Songs Musikfoerlag, Sweden/MCA, Inc., 1984.
Best-selling record by Murray Head from the album *Chess* (RCA, 85). As he did with "Jesus Christ Superstar," Murray Head introduced a song from a play before its opening, in this case *Chess* scheduled for 1986 in England.

One Night Love Affair (Canadian)
Words and music by Bryan Adams and Jim Vallance.
Adams Communications, Inc., 1984/Calypso Toonz, 1984/Irving Music Inc., 1984.
Best-selling record by Bryan Adams from the album *Reckless* (A & M, 85).

One of the Living
Words and music by Holly Knight.
Makiki Publishing Co., Ltd., 1985/Arista Music, Inc., 1985.
Introduced by Tina Turner in the film *Mad Max Beyond Thunderdome* (85). Best-selling record by Tina Turner (Capitol, 85).

One Owner Heart
Words and music by Walt Aldridge, Tom Brasfield, and Mac McAnally.
Rick Hall Music, 1984/Beginner Music, 1984/Tom Brasfield Music, 1984.
Best-selling record by T. G. Sheppard from the album *Livin' on the Edge* (Warner Bros., 85).

One Silk Sheet
Words by Marc Elliott, music by Larry Hochman.
Ba-Ba-Do Music, 1985.
Introduced by James Lecesne in the musical *One Man Band* (85).

One Vision (English)
Words by Queen.
Queen Music Ltd., 1985/Beechwood Music Corp.
Introduced by Queen (Capitol, 85) in the film *Iron Eagle* (85).

One Way Love (Better Off Dead)
Words and music by Steve Goldstein, Duane Hitchings, Craig Krampf, and Eric Nelson.
Irving Music Inc., 1985/Blackwood Music Inc., 1985/Almo Music Corp., 1985/April Music, Inc., 1985.
Introduced by E. G. Daily in the film *Better Off Dead* (85).

Only the Young
Words and music by Steve Perry, Neal Schon, and Jonathan Cain.
Twist & Shout Music, 1983/Weed High Nightmare Music/Colgems-EMI Music Inc.
Best-selling record by Journey (Warner Bros., 85). Featured in the film *Vision Quest* (83) and its soundtrack album. Introduced by Patty Smyth and Scandal in 1985 on the LP *The Warrior* (Columbia, 84).

Operator
Words and music by Boaz Watson, Vincent Calloway, Belinda Lipscomb, and Reggie Calloway.
Hip-Trip Music Co., 1984/Midstar Music, Inc.
Best-selling record by Midnight Star from the album *Planetary Invasion* (Elektra, 85).

Out of Touch
See *Popular Music, 1980-1984.*

Outta the World
Words and music by Nick Ashford and Valerie Simpson.
Nick-O-Val Music, 1984.
Best-selling record by Ashford and Simpson in 1985 from the album *Solid* (Capitol, 84).

P

Part-Time Lover
Words and music by Stevie Wonder.
Jobete Music Co., Inc., 1985/Black Bull Music, 1985.
Best-selling record by Stevie Wonder from the album *In Square Circle*
  (Motown, 85).

Party All the Time
Words and music by Rick James.
Stone City Music, 1985/National League Music, 1985.
Best-selling record by Eddie Murphy from the album *How Could It Be*
  (Columbia, 85), which marked the comedian's debut as a singer in his
  own right (rather than parodying other artists).

Peeping Tom
Words and music by Rockwell, Janet Cole, and Antoine Greene.
Jobete Music Co., Inc., 1985.
Introduced by Rockwell (Motown, 85). Featured in the film *The Last
  Dragon* (85).

Penny Lover
See *Popular Music, 1980-1984.*

People Are People
Words and music by Martin K. Gore.
Warner-Tamerlane Publishing Corp., 1985.
Best-selling record by Depeche Mode from the album *People Are People*
  (Warner Bros., 85).

People Get Ready
Revived by Jeff Beck and Rod Stewart on the album *Flash* (Epic, 85).
  See *Popular Music, 1920-1979.*

Percy's Song
Words and music by Bob Dylan.
Warner Brothers, Inc., 1963.

Released by Bob Dylan for the first time on the five-record retrospective *Biograph* (Columbia, 85).

Perfect Way (English)
Words and music by Green Strohmeyer-Gartside and David Gamson.
Jouissance, England, 1985/David Gamson, England, 1985/WB Music Corp., 1985.
Best-selling record by Scritti Politti from the album *Cupid and Psyche 85* (Warner Bros., 85).

A Picture of Lisa
Words and music by N. S. Leibowitz and George Feltenstein.
N. S. Leibowitz & George Feltenstein, 1985.
Introduced by Matthew McClanahan in the musical *Attack of the Killer Revue* (85).

A Place to Fall Apart
Words and music by Merle Haggard, Willie Nelson, and Freddy Powers.
Mount Shasta Music Inc., 1984.
Best-selling record by Merle Haggard from the album *Merle Haggard's Epic Hits* (Epic, 85).

Pop Life
Words and music by Prince Rogers Nelson.
Controversy Music, 1985.
Best-selling record by Prince & The Revolution from the album *Around the World in a Day* (Warner Bros., 85).

Porn Wars
Words and music by Frank Zappa.
Munchkin Music, 1985.
Introduced by Frank Zappa on the album *Frank Zappa Meets the Mothers of Prevention* (Barking Pumpkin, 85). Zappa emerged as a leader in pop music's fight against the censorship the industry feared when a group of women, some married to federal legislators and administrators—hence the name, Coalition of Washington Wives—proposed rating records according to their lyrics and posting parental warning stickers on those they disapproved. Zappa answers such critics in this song.

The Power of Love
Words and music by Chris Hayes, Huey Lewis, and Johnny Colla.
Hulex Music, 1985/Red Admiral Music Inc.
Best-selling record by Huey Lewis & The News (Chrysalis, 85). Introduced in the film *Back to the Future* (85). Nominated for an Academy

Award, Song of the Year, 1985; a National Academy of Recording Arts and Sciences Award, Record of the Year, 1985.

Private Dancer
Words and music by Mark Knopfler.
Almo Music Corp., 1984.
Best-selling record by Tina Turner in 1985 from the album *Private Dancer* (Capitol, 84).

Putting It Together
Words and music by Stephen Sondheim.
Revelation Music Publishing Corp., 1984/Rilting Music Inc., 1984.
Revived by Barbra Streisand on *The Broadway Album* (Columbia, 85). Song was introduced in 1984 in the musical *Sunday in the Park With George* and extensively rewritten for Streisand to perform.

R

Radio Heart
Words and music by Steve Davis and Dennis Morgan.
Tapadero Music, 1984/Tom Collins Music Corp., 1984.
Best-selling record by Charly McClain from the album *Radio Heart*
  (Epic, 85).

Rain Forest (English)
Words and music by Paul Hardcastle.
Oval Music Co., 1985/Virgin Music, Inc., 1985.
Best-selling record by Paul Hardcastle from the album *Rain Forest*
  (Chrysalis, 85).

Raspberry Beret
Words and music by Prince Rogers Nelson.
Controversy Music, 1985.
Best-selling record by Prince & The Revolution from the album *Around
  the World in a Day* (Warner Bros., 85).

Red Roses (Won't Work Now)
Words and music by Jimbeau Hinson and David Murphy.
Goldrian Music, 1984/N2D Publishing, 1984.
Introduced by Reba McEntire on the album *Have I Got a Deal for You*
  (MCA, 85).

Relax (English)
Words and music by William Johnson, Mark O'Toole, and Peter
  Gill.
Island Music, 1984.
Best-selling record by Frankie Goes to Hollywood from the album *Wel-
  come to the Pleasure Dome* (ZTT/Island, 85).

Remo's Theme: What If?
Words and music by Tommy Shaw and Richie Cannata.
Tranquility Base Songs, 1985.

Best-selling record by Tommy Shaw (A & M, 85). Introduced in the film *Remo Williams: The Adventure Begins* (85).

Restless Heart
Words and music by John Waite.
Alley Music, 1984.
Best-selling record by John Waite in 1985 from the album *No Brakes* (EMI-America, 84).

Rhythm of the Night
Words and music by Diane Warren.
Edition Sunset Publishing Inc., 1984/Arista Music, Inc., 1984.
Best-selling record by DeBarge from the album *Rhythm of the Night* (Motown, 85). Introduced in the film *The Last Dragon* (85).

The Riddle (English)
Words and music by Nik Kershaw.
Irving Music Inc., 1984.
Introduced by Nik Kershaw on the album *The Riddle* (MCA, 85).

Right from the Heart
Words and music by Earl Rose and Kathleen Wakefield.
American Broadcasting Music, Inc., 1985/Amadeus Music Co., 1985/April Music, Inc., 1985/Lady of the Lakes Music, 1985.
Introduced by Johnny Mathis on the soap opera *Ryan's Hope* (85). Performed by Johnny Mathis on the album *Right from the Heart* (Columbia, 85).

River Deep, Mountain High
See *Popular Music, 1920-1979*. Performed by Darlene Love in the Broadway musical *Leader of the Pack* (85), which was based on the life of songwriter Ellie Greenwich and included many of her songs from the 1960's. Love was the lead singer on many of legendary producer Phil Spector's finest recordings of that era.

River in the Rain
Words and music by Roger Miller.
Roger Miller Music, 1985/Tree Publishing Co., Inc., 1985.
Introduced by Daniel Jenkins and Ron Richardson in the musical *Big River* (85).

Road to Nowhere
Words by David Byrne, music by Chris Frantz, Tina Weymouth, and Jerry Harrison.
Index Music, 1985/Bleu Disque Music, 1985.
Best-selling record by The Talking Heads from the album *Little Creatures* (Sire, 85).

Rock and Roll Girls
Words and music by John Fogerty.
Wenaha Music Co., 1984.
Best-selling record by John Fogerty from the album *Centerfield* (Warner Bros., 85).

Rock Me Tonight (for Old Times Sake)
Words and music by Paul Laurence (pseudonym for Paul Laurence Jones).
Paul Laurence Jones, III, 1985/Bush Burnin' Music, 1985.
Best-selling record by Freddie Jackson from the album *Rock Me Tonight* (Capitol, 85).

Rock of Rages
Words and music by Ellie Greenwich and Jeff Kent.
My Own Music, 1985/Jent Music Inc., 1985.
Introduced by Dinah Manoff in the musical *Leader of the Pack* (Elektra/ Asylum, 85).

Roxanne, Roxanne
Words and music by Curtis Bedeau, Frederick Reeves, Lucien George, Brian George, Paul George, Hugh Clarke, Jeffrey Campbell, Gerard Charles, and Shaun Fequiere.
Kadoc Music, 1984/Mokajumbi, 1984/Adra Music, 1984.
Best-selling record by UTFO (Select, 85). Originally a B-side, this song was discovered in the discos of New York City and inspired a number of response records including "Roxanne's Revenge," "Roxanne's Doctor - The Real Man," "Queen of Rox (Shante-Rox On)," "Sparky's Turn (Roxanne You're Thru)," "Roxanne's a Man (The Untold Story)," and "The Real Roxanne."

Run to You (Canadian)
Words and music by Bryan Adams and Jim Vallance.
Adams Communications, Inc., 1984/Calypso Toonz, 1984/Irving Music Inc., 1984.
Best-selling record by Bryan Adams from the album *Reckless* (A & M, 85).

Runaway, Go Home
Words and music by Larry Gatlin.
Larry Gatlin Music, 1985.
Best-selling record by Larry Gatlin & The Gatlin Brothers Band from the album *Smile* (Columbia, 85).

Running up That Hill (English)
Words and music by Kate Bush.

Colgems-EMI Music Inc., 1985.
Best-selling record by Kate Bush from the album *Hounds of Love* (EMI-America, 85).

S

St. Elmo's Fire (Man in Motion)
Words and music by David Foster and John Parr.
Gold Horizon Music Corp., 1985/Foster Frees Music Inc., 1985/
   Carbert Music Inc., 1985/Golden Torch Music Corp., 1985.
Best-selling record by John Parr (Atlantic, 85). Introduced in the film
   St. Elmo's Fire; performed on its soundtrack album.

Sally (English)
Words and music by Sade Adu, music by Stuart Matthewman.
Silver Angel Music Inc., 1985.
Introduced by Sade on the album *Diamond Life* (Epic, 85).

Sanctified Lady
Words and music by Marvin Gaye and Gordon Banko.
April Music, Inc., 1985/Connie's Bank of Music, 1985.
Best-selling record by Marvin Gaye from the album *Dream of a Lifetime*
   (Columbia).

Santa Claus Is Coming to Town
Revived by Bruce Springsteen on the B-Side of "My Hometown" (Columbia, 85). See *Popular Music, 1920-1979.*

Santa Claus Is Watching You
Words and music by Ray Stevens.
Lowery Music Co., Inc., 1985.
Introduced by Ray Stevens on the album *I Have Returned* (MCA, 85).

Save a Prayer (English)
Words and music by Duran Duran.
Tritec Music Ltd., England, 1982.
Best-selling record by Duran Duran in 1985 from the album *Rio* (Capi-
   tol, 83). A live concert version of this song is included on the group's
   album *Arena* (Capitol, 84).

Save Your Love (for Number 1)
Words and music by Rene Moore and Angela Winbush.
A La Mode Music, 1985.
Best-selling record by Rene and Angela from the album *Street Called Desire* (Mercury, 85).

Saving All My Love for You
Words and music by Michael Masser and Gerry Goffin.
Prince Street Music, 1978/Screen Gems-EMI Music Inc.
Best-selling record by Whitney Houston from the album *Whitney Houston* (Arista, 85).

Say You, Say Me (Title Song from *White Nights*)
Words and music by Lionel Richie.
Brockman Enterprises Inc., 1985.
Best-selling record by Lionel Richie (Motown, 85). Introduced in the film *White Nights* (85). Won an Academy Award, Song of the Year, 1985.

Sea of Love
Revived by The Honeydrippers (Es Paranza, 84). See *Popular Music, 1920-1979.*

The Search Is Over
Words and music by Frankie Sullivan and Jim Peterik.
Rude Music, 1984/Easy Action Music.
Best-selling record by Survivor in 1985 from the album *Vital Signs* (Epic, 84).

Seeds
Words and music by Bruce Springsteen.
Bruce Springsteen Publishing, 1985.
Introduced by Bruce Springsteen on his 1984-85 tour, dedicated to displaced oil workers of Houston, Texas.

Sentimental Street
Words and music by Jack Blades and Francis Fitzgerald.
Kid Bird Music, 1985.
Best-selling record by Night Ranger from the album *Seven Wishes* (MCA, 85).

Separate Lives (Love Theme from *White Nights*)
Words and music by Stephen Bishop.
Stephen Bishop Music Publishing Co., 1985/Gold Horizon Music Corp.
Best-selling record Phil Collins and Marilyn Martin (Atlantic, 85). Introduced in the film *White Nights* (85). Nominated for an Academy Award, Song of the Year, 1985.

September Song
Revived by Lou Reed on the album *Lost in the Stars: The Music of Kurt Weill* (A & M, 85). See *Popular Music, 1920-1979.*

Seven Spanish Angels
Words and music by Troy Seals and Eddie Setser.
Warner-Tamerlane Publishing Corp., 1984/WB Music Corp., 1984/ Two-Sons Music, 1984.
Best-selling record by Ray Charles with Willie Nelson from the album *Friendship* (Columbia, 85).

Seven Summers
Words and music by Tito Larriva.
Placa Music, 1985.
Introduced by Cruzados on the album *Cruzados* (Arista, 85).

She Keeps the Home Fires Burning
Words and music by Dennis Morgan, Don Pfrimmer, and Mike Reid.
Tom Collins Music Corp., 1985/Collins Court Music, Inc./Lodge Hall Music, Inc.
Best-selling record by Ronnie Milsap from the album *Greatest Hits, Vol. 2* (RCA, 85) .

She Said the Same Things to Me
Words and music by John Hiatt.
Lillybilly, 1985.
Introduced by John Hiatt on the album *Warming Up to the Ice Age* (Geffen, 85).

She Twists the Knife Again (English)
Words and music by Richard Thompson.
Island Music, 1985.
Introduced by Richard Thompson on the album *Across a Crowded Room* (Mercury, 85).

She's a Miracle
Words and music by James Pennington and Sonny Lemaire.
Tree Publishing Co., Inc., 1984/Careers Music Inc., 1984.
Best-selling record by Exile from the album *Hang onto Your Heart* (Epic, 85).

She's Single Again
Words and music by Charlie Craig and Peter McCann.
Blackwood Music Inc., 1985/April Music, Inc., 1985/New & Used Music, 1985.
Best-selling record by Janie Fricke from the album *Somebody Else's Fire* (Columbia, 85).

(Come on) Shout
Words and music by Marti Sharron and Gary Skardina.
Welbeck Music Corp., 1985/Anidraks Music/Girl Productions.
Introduced by Alex Brown in the film *Girls Just Want to Have Fun* (85);
inspired by Cyndi Lauper's song of the same title.

Shout (English)
Words and music by Roland Orzabal and Ian Stanley.
Nymph Music, 1985.
Best-selling record by Tears for Fears from the album *Songs from the
Big Chair* (Mercury, 85).

Silent Running (English)
Words and music by Mike Rutherford and Brian Robertson.
Mike Rutherford, England, 1985/Pun Music Inc., London, England,
1985/B.A.R., England, 1985/WB Music Corp., 1985.
Best-selling record by Mike & The Mechanics from the album *Mike &
The Mechanics* (Atlantic, 85).

Singin' a Song
Words by Marc Elliott, music by Larry Hochman.
Ba-Ba-Do Music, 1985.
Introduced by Kay Cole, Judy Gibson, and Vanessa Williams in the
musical *One Man Band* (85).

Single Life
Words and music by Larry Blackmon and Thomas Jenkins.
All Seeing Eye Music, 1985/Larry Junior Music, 1985.
Best-selling record by Cameo from the album *Single Life* (Polygram, 85).

Sisters Are Doin' It for Themselves (English)
Words and music by Annie Lennox and Dave Stewart.
RCA Music Ltd., London, England, 1985/Blue Network Music Inc.,
1985.
Best-selling record by Eurythmics and Aretha Franklin from the albums
Be Yourself Tonight (RCA, 85) and *Who's Zoomin' Who* (Arista, 85).

Sleeping Bag
Words and music by Billy Gibbons, Dusty Hill, and Frank Beard.
Hamstein Music, 1985.
Best-selling record by ZZ Top from the album *Afterburner* (Warner
Bros., 85).

Small Blue Thing
Words and music by Suzanne Vega.
Waifersongs Ltd., 1985.
Introduced by Suzanne Vega on the album *Suzanne Vega* (A & M, 85).

Small Town
Words and music by John Cougar Mellencamp.
Riva Music Ltd., 1985.
Best-selling record by John Cougar Mellencamp from the album *Scare-crow* (Riva, 85).

Small Town Boy (English)
Words and music by Jimmy Somerville, Larry Steinbachek, and
Steve Bronski.
Bronski Music Ltd., England, 1984/William A. Bong Ltd., England,
1984.
Best-selling record by Bronski Beat from the album *The Age of Consent*
(MCA, 85). As opposed to John Cougar Mellencamp's "Small Town"
which evokes a patriotic pride of place and American heritage, the
Bronski's song details the painful reality of growing up homosexual
in England.

Smokin' in the Boy's Room
Revived by Motley Crue on the album *Theatre of Pain* (Elektra, 85). See
See *Popular Music, 1920-1979*. Correct name for the author is Cub
Koda.

Smooth Operator (English)
Words and music by Helen Folasade Adu and St.John.
Stuart Matthewman, England, 1984/Silver Angel Music Inc., 1984.
Best-selling record by Sade from the album *Diamond Life* (Epic, 85).

Smuggler's Blues
Words and music by Glenn Frey and Jack Tempchin.
Red Cloud Music Co., 1984/Night River Publishing.
Best-selling record by Glenn Frey from the album *The Allnighter*
(MCA, 85). Featured on the television series *Miami Vice* in an episode
inspired by and featuring Glenn Frey and his songs; also used on the
album of music from the series.

So in Love
Words and music by OMD, words and music by Steve Hague.
Charisma Music Publishing Co., Ltd., England, 1985/Virgin Music
Ltd., 1985/Unforgettable Songs, 1985/Unichappell Music Inc.,
1985.
Introduced by Orchestral Manoeuvres in the Dark from the album
Crush (A & M, 85).

Solid
Words and music by Nick Ashford and Valerie Simpson.
Nick-O-Val Music, 1984.

Best-selling record by Ashford and Simpson in 1985 from the album *Solid* (Capitol, 84).

Some Fools Never Learn
Words and music by John Sherrill.
Sweet Baby Music, 1982.
Best-selling record by Steve Wariner from the album *One Good Night Deserves Another* (MCA, 85).

Some Like It Hot
Words and music by Robert Palmer, Andy Taylor, and John Taylor.
Biot Music Ltd., Birmingham, England, 1985/Tritec Music Ltd., England, 1985/Bungalow Music, N.V., 1985/Ackee Music Inc., 1985.
Best-selling record by The Power Station from the album *The Power Station* (Capitol, 85).

Some Things Are Better Left Unsaid
Words and music by Daryl Hall.
Hot Cha Music Co., 1984/Unichappell Music Inc.
Best-selling record by Daryl Hall and John Oates in 1985 from the album *Big Bam Boom* (RCA, 84).

Somebody (Canadian)
Words and music by Bryan Adams and Jim Vallance.
Adams Communications, Inc., 1985/Calypso Toonz, 1985/Irving Music Inc., 1985.
Best-selling record by Bryan Adams from the album *Reckless* (A & M, 85).

Somebody Should Leave
Words and music by Harlan Howard and Chick Rains.
Tree Publishing Co., Inc., 1984/Choskee Bottom Music, 1984/Cross Keys Publishing Co., Inc., 1984.
Best-selling record by Reba McEntire from the album *Have I Got a Deal for You* (MCA, 85).

Something in My Heart
Words and music by Wayland Patton.
Jack & Bill Music Co., 1984.
Best-selling record by Ricky Skaggs from the album *Country Boy* (Epic, 85).

Somewhere I Belong
Words by Dean Pitchford, music by Marvin Hamlisch.
Famous Music Corp., 1985/Ensign Music Corp., 1985.
Introduced by Teddy Pendergrass in the film *Daryl* (85).

Song for the Dreamers
Words and music by Dan Stuart and Steve Wynn.
Poisoned Brisket Music, 1985/Hang Dog Music, 1985.
Introduced by Danny and Dusty on the album *The Lost Weekend* (A
& M, 85).

Song for the Poor
Words and music by John Michael Talbot.
Birdwing Music, 1985.
Best-selling record by various artists (Lamb & Lion, 85). The recording
by Gospel singers to raise money for Ethiopian famine victims fea-
tured Debby Boone, Pat Boone, Tata Vega, and John Michael Talbot.

Soul Kiss
Words and music by Mark Goldenberg.
Music Corp. of America, 1985.
Best-selling record by Olivia Newton-John from the album *Soul Kiss*
(MCA, 85).

Spanish Eddie, see **The Night Spanish Eddie Cashed It In.**

Spies Like Us
Words and music by Paul McCartney.
MPL Communications Inc., 1985.
Introduced by Paul McCartney in the film *Spies Like Us* (85).

Steady
Words and music by Jules Shear and Cyndi Lauper.
Funzalo Music/Reilla Music Corp., 1983.
Introduced by by Jules Shear on the album *The Eternal Return* (EMI-
America, 85).

Step That Step
Words and music by Mark Miller.
GID Music Inc., 1983.
Best-selling record by Sawyer Brown from the album *Sawyer Brown*
(Capitol, 85).

Stir It Up
Words and music by Allee Willis and Michael Sembello.
Unicity Music, Inc., 1984/Off Backstreet Music, 1984.
Introduced by Patti LaBelle in the film *Beverly Hills Cop* (85); used on
its soundtrack album.

Suddenly
Words and music by Keith Diamond and Billy Ocean.
Zomba Enterprises, Inc., 1984/Willesden Music, Inc., 1984.

Best-selling record by Billy Ocean in 1985 from the album *Suddenly* (Arista, 84).

Sugar Walls
Words and music by Alexander Nevermind (pseudonym for Prince Rogers Nelson).
Tionna Music, 1984.
Best-selling record by Sheena Easton in 1985 from the album *A Private Heaven* (EMI-America, 84). Song frequently cited as having lyrics as among the steamiest of the year.

Summer of '69 (Canadian)
Words and music by Bryan Adams and Jim Vallance.
Adams Communications, Inc., 1984/Calypso Toonz/Irving Music Inc.
Best-selling record by Bryan Adams from the album *Reckless* (A & M, 85).

Sun City
Words and music by Steven Van Zandt.
Solidarity, 1985.
Best-selling record by Artists United Against Apartheid from the album *Sun City* (Capitol, 85) which featured an all-star group of urban, rap, street, and pop musicians, and jazz great Miles Davis. This song calls upon musicians of all types to avoid performing in Sun City, a resort community frequented by whites from South Africa, in order to protest that country's policy of racial separation.

Sunset Grill
Words and music by Don Henley, Dan Kortchmar, and Ben Tench.
Cass County Music Co., 1984/Kortchmar Music, 1984.
Introduced by Don Henley on the album *Building the Perfect Beast* (Geffen, 85).

Surprise Surprise
Words by Edward Kleban, music by Marvin Hamlisch.
Wren Music Co., Inc., 1985/American Compass Music Corp., 1985.
Introduced by Greg Burge in the film *A Chorus Line* (85). This song was added to the score of the film version of the hit Broadway play. Nominated for an Academy Award, Song of the Year, 1985.

Sussudio (English)
Words and music by Phil Collins.
Pun Music Inc., London, England, 1985.
Best-selling record by Phil Collins from the album *No Jacket Required* (Atlantic, 85).

Sweet Dreams
Revived as the title track of the 1985 film *Sweet Dreams,* based on the
life story of country singer Patsy Cline, who had a hit record of the
song in 1963. See *Popular Music, 1920-1979.*

Sweet, Sweet Baby (I'm Falling)
Words and music by Maria McKee, Steve Van Zandt, and Ben
Tench.
Blue Midnight Music, 1985/Little Diva Music, 1985/Blue Gator
Music, 1985.
Introduced by Lone Justice on the album *Lone Justice* (Geffen, 85).

Swingin' Party
Words and music by Paul Westerberg.
NAH Music, 1985.
Introduced by The Replacements on the album *Tim* (Sire, 85).

T

Take on Me (Norwegian)
English words and music by Pal Weaktaar, Mags, and Marten Harket.
ATV Music Corp., 1985.
Best-selling record by A-Ha from the album *Hunting High and Low* (Warner Bros, 85).

Take the Skinheads Bowling
Words and music by Camper Van Beethoven.
N. S. Leibowitz & George Feltenstein, 1985.
Introduced by Camper Van Beethoven on the album *Telephone Free Landslide Victory* (Indepdendent Project Records, 85).

Talk to Me
Words and music by Chas. Sandford.
Fallwater Music, 1985.
Best-selling record by Stevie Nicks from the album *Rock a Little* (Modern, 85).

Tell Me on a Sunday (English)
Words by Don Black, music by Andrew Lloyd Webber.
Dick James Music Inc., 1980.
Introduced by Marti Webb in the British musical *Tell Me on a Sunday.* Performed by Bernadette Peters in the Broadway musical *Song and Dance* (85).

Temporary Insanity
Words and music by L. White, M. Rochelle, and S. Berry.
National League Music, 1985/Gedzerillo Music, 1985/Bullwhip Productions, 1985/WB Music Corp., 1985.
Introduced by Townsends in the film *Police Academy II* (85).

That Was Yesterday
Words and music by Mick Jones and Lou Gramm.
Somerset Songs Publishing, Inc., 1984/Evansongs Ltd., 1984/Stray

Notes Music, 1984.
Best-selling record by Foreigner from the album *Agent Provocateur* (Atlantic, 85).

That's What Friends Are For
Words by Carole Bayer Sager, music by Bert Bacharach.
WB Music Corp., 1985/New Hidden Valley Music Co., 1985/
  Warner-Tamerlane Publishing Corp., 1985/Carole Bayer Sager
  Music, 1985.
Best-selling record by Dionne Warwick with Elton John, Gladys Knight, and Stevie Wonder from the album *Friends* (Arista, 85). Proceeds donated to the American Foundation for AIDS Research. Introduced in the film *Nightshift* in 1982.

Theme from *Mr. Belvedere*
Words and music by Gary Portnoy and Judy-Hart Angelo.
Addax Music Co., Inc., 1985.
Introduced by Leon Redbone on the television series *Mr. Belvedere* (85).

There's No Way
Words and music by Lisa Palas, Will Robinson, and John Jarrard.
Alabama Band Music Co., 1984.
Best-selling record by Alabama from the album *40 Hour Week* (RCA, 85).

Thing about You
Words and music by Tom Petty.
Gone Gator Music, 1982.
Featured in *Southern Pacific* (Warner Bros.).

Things Can Only Get Better (English)
Words and music by Howard Jones.
Warner-Tamerlane Publishing Corp., 1985.
Best-selling record by Howard Jones from the album *Dream into Action* (Elektra, 85).

Thinking About Your Love
Words and music by Rodney Skipworth and Phil Turner.
Larry Spier, Inc., 1985.
Introduced by Skipworth and Turner in the film *Pumping Iron II: The Women* (85).

This Is Not America
Words and music by Pat Metheny and Lyle Mays.
Buttermilk Sky Music, 1985/OPC, 1985.
Best-selling record by David Bowie and Pat Metheny (EMI-America, 85). Introduced in the film *The Falcon and the Snowman* (85).

Through the Fire
Words and music by David Foster, Tom Keane, and Cynthia Weil.
Foster Frees Music Inc., 1984/Dyad Music, Ltd., 1984/TomJon
    Music, 1984/NeroPublishing, 1984.
Best-selling record by Chaka Khan from the album *I Feel for You*
    (Warner Bros., 85). Nominated for a National Academy of Recording
    Arts and Sciences Award, Rhythm 'n Blues Song of the Year, 1985.

Tight Connection to My Heart (Has Anybody Seen My Love)
Words and music by Bob Dylan.
Special Rider Music, 1985.
Best-selling record by Bob Dylan from the album *Empire Burlesque*
    (Columbia, 85).

'Til My Baby Comes Home
Words and music by Luther Vandross and Marcus Miller.
April Music, Inc., 1985/Uncle Ronnie's Music Co., Inc., 1985/
    Thriller Miller Music, 1985/MCA, Inc., 1985.
Best-selling record by Luther Vandross from the album *The Night I Fell
    in Love* (Epic, 85).

Time Don't Run Out on Me
Words by Gerry Goffin, music by Carole King.
Screen Gems-EMI Music Inc., 1983/Elorac Music/Colgems-EMI
    Music Inc.
Best-selling record by Anne Murray from the album *Heart over Mind*
    (Capitol, 85).

To Live and Die in L.A.
Words and music by Wang Chung.
Chung Music Ltd., 1985.
Introduced by Wang Chung in the film *To Live and Die in L.A.* (85).

Tonight She Comes
Words and music by Ric Ocasek.
Lido Music Inc., 1985.
Best-selling record by The Cars from the album *Greatest Hits* (Elektra,
    85).

Too Late for Goodbyes (English)
Words and music by Julian Lennon.
Chappell & Co., Inc., 1984.
Best-selling record by Julian Lennon in 1985 from the album *Valotte*
    (Atlantic, 84). Author is the son of the late John Lennon.

Too Much on My Heart
Words and music by Lester Fortune.
Statler Brothers Music, 1985.

Best-selling record by The Statler Brothers from the album *Pardners in Rhyme* (Mercury, 85).

Touch a Hand, Make a Friend
Words and music by Homer Banks, Raymond Jackson, and Carl Hampton.
Irving Music Inc., 1985.
Best-selling record by The Oak Ridge Boys from the album *Step on Out* (MCA, 85).

Trapped
Words and music by Jimmy Cliff.
Island Music, 1972.
Recorded by Bruce Springsteen on the album *We Are the World* (Columbia, 85). Proceeds donated to the U.S.A. for Africa fund.

U

Under a Raging Moon (English)
Words and music by John Parr and Julia Downes.
Carbert Music Inc., 1985.
Best-selling record by Roger Daltrey from the album *Under a Raging Moon* (Atlantic, 85). This song is dedicated to the late Keith Moon, drummer of the rock group The Who, for which Daltrey was lead singer.

Unexpected Song (English)
Words by Don Black, music by Andrew Lloyd Webber.
Dick James Music Inc., 1982.
Performed by Bernadette Peters in the musical *Song and Dance* (85). Introduced in England in 1982.

Used to Blue
Words and music by Fred Knobloch and Bill LaBounty.
Montage Music Inc., 1985/Captain Crystal Music, 1985/A Little More Music Inc., 1985.
Best-selling record by Sawyer Brown from the album *Sawyer Brown* (Capitol, 85).

V

Vanz Can't Dance, see **Zanz Can't Dance.**

A View to a Kill (English)
Words and music by Duran Duran, music by John Barry.
Danjag, S.A., England, 1985/Tritec Music Ltd., England, 1985.
Best-selling record by Duran Duran (Capitol, 85). Introduced in the
    James Bond film *A View to a Kill* (85), which featured this group's
    first film soundtrack.

Voices Carry
Words and music by Aimee Mann, Michael Hausman, Robert
    Holmes, and Joseph Pesce.
Intersong, USA Inc., 1985/'Til Tunes Associates, 1985.
Best-selling record by 'Til Tuesday from the album *Voices Carry* (Epic,
    85). This title track was the group's first hit.

W

Wake Me Up Before You Go Go
See *Popular Music, 1980-1984.*

Wake Up (Next to You) (English)
Words and music by Graham Parker.
Ellisclar, England, 1985.
Best-selling record by Graham Parker from the album *Steady Nerves* (Elektra, 85).

Walk of Life (English)
Words and music by Mark Knopfler.
Almo Music Corp., 1985.
Best-selling record by Dire Straits from the album *Brothers in Arms* (Warner Bros., 85).

Walkin' a Broken Heart
Words and music by Alan Rush and Dennis Linde.
Combine Music Corp., 1983/Dennis Linde Music, 1983.
Best-selling record by Don Williams from *Greatest Hits IV* (MCA, 85).

Walking on Sunshine
Words and music by Kimberly Rew.
Screen Gems-EMI Music Inc., 1985.
Best-selling record by Katrina and the Waves from the album *Katrina and the Waves* (Capitol, 85).

Warning Sign
Words and music by Eddie Rabbitt and Even Stevens.
Debdave Music Inc., 1984/Briarpatch Music.
Best-selling record by Eddie Rabbitt from the album *The Best Year of My Life* (Warner Bros., 85).

The Way You Do the Things You Do
Revived by Daryl Hall and John Oates as part of a medley with "My

Girl" on the album *Hall and Oates Live at the Apollo* (RCA, 85). See *Popular Music, 1920-1979.*

Ways to Be Wicked
Words and music by Mike Campbell and Tom Petty.
Gone Gator Music, 1985/Wild Gator Music, 1985.
Best-selling record by Lone Justice from the album *Lone Justice* (Geffen, 85).

We Are the World
Words and music by Michael Jackson and Lionel Richie.
Mijac Music, 1985/Brockman Enterprises Inc.
Best-selling record by U.S.A. for Africa from the album *We Are the World* (Columbia, 85). Perhaps the most famous of the Ethiopian-aid songs, performed by a virtual hall of fame of the American pop music community, including Bob Dylan, Ray Charles, Bruce Springsteen, and Harry Belafonte. Won National Academy of Recording Arts and Sciences Awards, Record of the Year, 1985, and Song of the Year, 1985.

We Belong
See *Popular Music, 1980-1984.*

We Built This City
Words by Bernie Taupin, words and music by Martin Page, Dennis Lambert, and Peter Wolf.
Intersong, USA Inc., 1985/Little Mole Music, 1985/Zomba Enterprises, Inc., 1985/Petwolf Music, 1985/Tuneworks Music, 1985.
Best-selling record by Starship from the album *Knee Deep in the Hoopla* (RCA, 85).

We Don't Need Another Hero (Thunderdome)
Words and music by Terry Britten and Graham Lyle.
Myax Music Ltd., England, 1985/Good Single Ltd., England, 1985.
Best-selling record by Tina Turner (Capitol, 85). Introduced in the film *Mad Max: Beyond Thunderdome* (85).

Weird Science
Words and music by Danny Elfman.
Music Corp. of America, 1985.
Introduced by Oingo Boingo in the film *Weird Science* (85).

Welcome to the Pleasure Dome (English)
Words and music by William Johnson, Mark O'Toole, Peter Gill, and Brian Nash.
Island Music, 1984.

Best-selling record by Frankie Goes to Hollywood from the album *Welcome to the Pleasure Dome* (ZTT/Island, 85).

We're Gonna Make It (After All)
Words and music by Ellie Greenwich.
My Own Music, 1983.
Introduced by Ellie Greenwich in the musical *Leader of the Pack* (Elektra/Asylum, 85), which was based on her life story.

What a Thrill
Words and music by Cyndi Lauper and John Turi.
Warner-Tamerlane Publishing Corp., 1985.
Introduced by Cyndi Lauper on the B-Side of the single "Goonies 'R' Good Enough" (Portrait, 85). Co-author John Turi was a partner in Lauper's first group, Blue Angel.

What about Love? (Canadian)
Words and music by Sheron Alton, Brian Allen, and Jim Vallance.
Welbeck Music Corp., 1983/Irving Music Inc./Calypso Toonz.
Best-selling record by Heart from the album *Heart* (Capitol, 85).

What I Didn't Do
Words and music by Wood Newton and Michael Noble.
Warner House of Music, 1985/Bobby Goldsboro Music, 1985.
Best-selling record by Steve Warner from the album *One Good Night Deserves Another* (MCA, 85).

What Would I Do Without You
Words and music by Van Morrison.
Essential Music, 1985.
Introduced by Van Morrison on the album *A Sense of Wonder* (Mercury, 85).

What You See Is What You Get
Words and music by Charles Strouse.
Charles Strouse Music, 1985.
Introduced by Lenny Wolpe in the Off Broadway musical *Mayor* (85).

When Love Breaks Down (Irish)
Words and music by Paddy McAloon.
Blackwood Music Inc., 1985.
Introduced by Prefab Sprout on the album *Two Wheels Good* (Epic, 85).

When the Going Gets Tough the Tough Get Going
Words and music by Wayne Brathwaite, Barry Eastmond, Robert John Lange, and Billy Ocean.
Zomba Enterprises, Inc., 1985.

Best-selling record by Billy Ocean (Arista, 85). Introduced in the film *Jewel of the Nile* (85).

When the Spell Is Broken (English)
Words and music by Richard Thompson.
Island Music, 1985.
Introduced by Richard Thompson on the album *Across a Crowded Room* (Mercury, 85).

When We Ran
Words and music by John Hiatt.
Lillybilly, 1985.
Introduced by John Hiatt on the album *Warming Up to the Ice Age* (Geffen, 85).

When Your Heart Is Weak
Words and music by Peter Kingsbery.
Nurk Twins Music, 1984/Edwin Ellis Music, 1984.
Introduced by Cock Robin on the album *Cock Robin* (Columbia, 85).

Where Do the Children Go
Words and music by Rob Hyman and Eric Bazilian.
Human Boy Music, 1984/Dub Notes, 1984.
Introduced by by The Hooters on the album *Nervous Night* (Columbia, 85).

Where Do They Go
Words and music by Jerry Raney.
Cricket Pie Music, 1985.
Introduced by The Beat Farmers on the album *Tales of the New West* (Rhino, 85).

Who's Gonna Fill Their Shoes
Words and music by Troy Seals and M. D. Barnes.
WB Music Corp., 1985/Two-Sons Music, 1985/Tree Publishing Co., Inc., 1985.
Best-selling record by George Jones from the album *Who's Gonna Fill Their Shoes* (Epic, 85).

Who's Holding Donna Now
Words and music by David Foster, Jay Graydon, and Randy Goodrum.
Foster Frees Music Inc., 1985/Garden Rake Music, Inc./April Music, Inc./Random Notes.
Best-selling record by DeBarge from the album *Rhythm of the Night* (Motown, 85).

Who's Zoomin' Who
Words and music by Narada Michael Walden, Preston Glass, and Aretha Franklin.
Gratitude Sky Music, Inc., 1985/Bell Boy Music, 1985/Springtime Music Inc., 1985.
Best-selling record by Aretha Franklin from the album *Who's Zoomin' Who* (Arista, 85).

Why Worry? (English)
Words and music by Mark Knopfler.
Chariscourt Ltd., 1985/Almo Music Corp., 1985/Viva Music, Inc., 1985.
Introduced by Dire Straits on the album *Brothers in Arms* (Warner Bros., 85).

The Wild Boys
See *Popular Music, 1980-1984.*

Will the Wolf Survive
Words and music by David Hidalgo and Louie Perez.
Davince Music, 1984/No Ko Music, 1984.
Best-selling record by Los Lobos from the album *Will the Wolf Survive* (Warner Bros./Slash, 85).

Willie and the Hand Jive
Words and music by Johnny Otis.
Eldorado Music Co., 1958.
Revived by George Thorogood & The Destroyers on the album *Maverick* (EMI-America, 85).

Would I Lie to You? (English)
Words and music by Annie Lennox and Dave Stewart.
Blue Network Music Inc., 1985.
Best-selling record by Eurythmics from the album *Be Yourself Tonight* (RCA, 85).

Wrap Her Up (English)
Words and music by Davey Johnstone, Bernie Taupin, and Elton John.
Intersong, USA Inc., 1985.
Best-selling record by Elton John from the album *Ice on Fire* (Geffen, 85).

Y, Z

You Are My Lady
Words and music by Barry Eastmond.
Zomba Enterprises, Inc., 1985/Barry Eastmond Music, 1985.
Best-selling record by Freddie Jackson from the album *Rock Me Tonight* (Capitol, 85).

You Belong to the City
Words and music by Glenn Frey.
Red Cloud Music Co., 1985/Night River Publishing, 1985.
Best-selling record by Glenn Frey (MCA, 85). Featured on the season premier episode of the television series *Miami Vice* (85) and on the show's soundtrack album.

You Don't Say (English)
Words and music by Richard Thompson.
Island Music, 1985.
Introduced by Richard Thompson on the album *Across a Crowded Room* (Mercury, 85).

You Give Good Love
Words and music by LaForrest "La La" Cope.
MCA, Inc., 1985/New Music Group, 1985.
Best-selling record by Whitney Houston from the album *Whitney Houston* (Arista, 85). Nominated for a National Academy of Recording Arts and Sciences Award, Rhythm 'n Blues Song of the Year, 1985.

You Look Marvelous
Words by Billy Crystal, music by Paul Shaffer.
Billy Crystal & Paul Shaffer, 1985/New Music Group, 1985/ Postvalda Music, 1985.
Best-selling record by comedian Billy Crystal from the album *You Look Marvelous* (A & M, 85). The record is based on one of Crystal's featured characterizations on the television show *Saturday Night Live*.

You Make Me Want to Make You Mine
Words and music by Dave Loggins.
Leeds Music Corp., 1985/Patchwork Music.
Best-selling record by Juice Newton from the album *Old Flame* (RCA, 85).

You Spin Me Round (Like a Record)
Words and music by Peter Burns, Steven Coy, Timothy Lever, and Michael Percy.
Chappell & Co., Inc., 1985.
Best-selling record by Dead or Alive from the album *Youthquake* (Epic, 85); perhaps the top dance track of the year.

You Wear It Well
Words and music by Chico DeBarge and Eldra DeBarge.
Jobete Music Co., Inc., 1985.
Best-selling record by El DeBarge with DeBarge from the album *Rhythm of the Night* (Motown, 85).

You're the Inspiration
Words and music by Peter Cetera and David Foster.
Double Virgo Music, 1984/Foster Frees Music Inc.
Best-selling record by Chicago from the album *Chicago XVII* (Warner Bros., 85).

Zanz Can't Dance, also known as **Vanz Can't Dance**
Words and music by John Fogerty.
Wenaha Music, 1984.
Introduced by John Fogerty on the album *Centerfield* (Warner Bros., 85). Fogerty was sued for libel over this song by his former boss, Sol Zaentz, president of Fantasy Records, who claimed that the dancing pig in the lyric, who was also a pickpocket, was a slanderous portrayal. The song was later retitled "Vanz Can't Dance."

Indexes and List of Publishers

Lyricists & Composers Index

Lyricists & Composers Index

Lyricists & Composers Index

Lyricists & Composers Index

Lyricists & Composers Index

Freedom
I'm Your Man
Midnight, Charlie
   Name of the Game
Miller, B.
   The Last Dragon
Miller, Frankie
   Lie to You for Your Love
Miller, Marcus
   'Til My Baby Comes Home
Miller, Mark
   Step That Step
Miller, Roger
   Muddy Water
   River in the Rain
Mills, Mike
   Can't Get There from Here
Mitchell, Joni
   Good Friends
   Impossible Dreamer
   Lucky Girl
Moore, Rene
   Save Your Love (for Number 1)
Morgan, Dennis
   Radio Heart
   She Keeps the Home Fires Burning
Moroder, Giorgio
   Never Ending Story
Morris, Gary
   Baby Bye Bye
Morrison, Brian
   Don't Call Him a Cowboy
Morrison, Van
   What Would I Do Without You
Morrissey, Tommy
   How Soon Is Now
   Meat Is Murder
Morrow, Marvin
   The Beast in Me
Murphy, David
   Red Roses (Won't Work Now)
Nash, Brian
   Welcome to the Pleasure Dome
Nelson, Eric
   One Way Love (Better Off Dead)
Nelson, Prince Rogers, *see also*
   Nevermind, Alexander
   I Would Die 4 U
   Jungle Love
   A Love Bizarre

Pop Life
Raspberry Beret
Nelson, Willie
   Forgiving You Was Easy
   A Place to Fall Apart
Nevermind, Alexander
   Sugar Walls
Newton, Wood
   What I Didn't Do
Nichol, Steve
   Hangin' on a String
Noble, Michael
   What I Didn't Do
Ocasek, Ric
   Tonight She Comes
Ocean, Billy
   Lover Boy
   Mystery Lady
   Suddenly
   When the Going Gets Tough the
     Tough Get Going
Omartian, Michael
   Closest Thing to Perfect
OMD
   So in Love
Orange, Walter
   Nightshift
Orzabal, Roland
   Shout
Orzabal, Roy
   Everybody Wants to Rule the World
Otis, Johnny
   Willie and the Hand Jive
O'Toole, Mark
   Relax
   Welcome to the Pleasure Dome
Overstreet, Paul
   I Fell in Love Again Last Night
Pack, David
   All I Need
Page, Martin
   We Built This City
Page, Richard
   Broken Wings
Palas, Lisa
   There's No Way
Palmer, David
   The Night Spanish Eddie Cashed It
     In

126

Lyricists & Composers Index

Lyricists & Composers Index

Important Performances Index

Songs are listed under the works in which they were introduced or given significant renditions. The index is organized into major sections by performance medium: Album, Movie, Musical, Revue, Television Show.

Album

Across a Crowded Room
  She Twists the Knife Again
  When the Spell Is Broken
  You Don't Say
Afterburner
  Sleeping Bag
The Age of Consent
  Small Town Boy
Agent Provocateur
  Down on Love
  I Want to Know What Love Is
  That Was Yesterday
Aimless Love
  The Bottomless Lake
  Maureen, Maureen
Air Supply
  Just As I Am
All for Love
  Count Me Out
All I Need
  All I Need
All Over the Place
  Hero Takes a Fall

The Allnighter
  Smuggler's Blues
Amber Waves of Grain
  Amber Waves of Grain
Animotion
  Let Him Go
  Obsession
Another World
  Love Radiates Around
  Love to See You
Anything Goes
  Baby Bye Bye
  I'll Never Stop Loving You
Arena
  Save a Prayer
Around the World in a Day
  Pop Life
  Raspberry Beret
Arrive Without Travelling
  Mrs. Green
Barking at Airplanes
  Crazy in the Night (Barking at Airplanes)
Be Yourself Tonight
  Sisters Are Doin' It for Themselves

134

Important Performances Index — Album

137

Movie

Important Performances Index — Movie

Stick
  I Don't Think I'm Ready for You
Sweet Dreams
  Sweet Dreams
Sylvester
  Breakaway
To Live and Die in L.A.
  To Live and Die in L.A.
A View to a Kill
  A View to a Kill
Vision Quest
  Crazy for You
  Curves
  Only the Young
Weird Science
  Weird Science
White Nights
  Say You, Say Me (Title Song from
    White Nights)
  Separate Lives (Love Theme from
    White Nights)
The Woman in Red
  Love Light in Flight

Musical
Attack of the Killer Revue
  A Picture of Lisa
Big River
  Muddy Water
  River in the Rain
Leader of the Pack
  Keep It Confidential
  River Deep, Mountain High
  Rock of Rages
  We're Gonna Make It (After All)
Mayor
  Central Park Ballad
  How'm I Doin'
  March of the Yuppies
  What You See Is What You Get
The Mystery of Edwin Drood
  The Garden Path to Hell
  Moonfall
One Man Band
  One Silk Sheet
  Singin' a Song
Song and Dance
  I Have Never Felt This Way Before

Tell Me on a Sunday
  Unexpected Song
Sunday in the Park With George
  Putting It Together
Tales of Tinseltown
  Jungle Fever
Tell Me on a Sunday
  Tell Me on a Sunday

Television Show
Growing Pains
  As Long as We Got Each Other
Miami Vice
  Miami Vice Theme
  Smuggler's Blues
  You Belong to the City
Mr. Belvedere
  Theme from Mr. Belvedere
Ryan's Hope
  Right from the Heart
Saturday Night Live
  You Look Marvelous
Vietnam Requiem
  19

141

Awards Index

A list of songs nominated for Academy Awards by the Academy of Motion Picture Arts and Sciences and Grammy Awards from the National Academy of Recording Arts and Sciences. Asterisks indicate the winners.

1985

Academy Award
  Miss Celie's Blues (Sisters)
  The Power of Love
  Say You, Say Me (Title Song from *White Nights*)*
  Separate Lives (Love Theme from *White Nights*)
  Surprise Surprise

National Academy of Recording Arts and Sciences Award
  Baby's Got Her Blue Jeans On
  Born in the U.S.A.
  The Boys of Summer
  Desperados Waiting for a Train
  Every Time You Go Away
  40 Hour Week (for a Livin')
  Freeway of Love*
  Highwayman*
  I Don't Know Why You Don't Want Me
  I Feel for You
  I Want to Know What Love Is
  Lost in the Fifties Tonight (In the Still of the Night)
  Love Is Alive
  Money for Nothing
  New Attitude
  Nightshift
  The Power of Love
  Through the Fire
  We Are the World*
  You Give Good Love

List of Publishers

A directory to publishers of the songs included in *Popular Music 1985*. Publishers that are members of the American Society of Composers, Authors, and Publishers or whose catalogs are available under ASCAP license are indicated by the designation (ASCAP). Publishers that have granted performing rights to Broadcast Music, Inc., are designated by the notation (BMI). Publishers whose catalogs are represented by SESAC, Inc., are indicated by the designation (SESAC).

The addresses were gleaned from a variety of sources, including ASCAP, BMI, SESAC, The Harry Fox Agency, *Billboard* magazine, and the National Music Publishers' Association. As in any volatile industry, many of the addresses may become quickly outdated. In the interim between the book's completion and its subsequent publication, some publishers may have been consolidated into others or changed hands. This is a fact of life long endured by the music business and its constituents. The data collected here, and throughout the book, are as accurate as such circumstances allow.

A

ABKCO Music Inc. (BMI)
1700 Broadway
New York, New York 10019

Ackee Music Inc. (ASCAP)
see Island Music

Acuff-Rose Publications Inc. (BMI)
2510 Franklin Road
Nashville, Tennessee 37204

Adams Communications, Inc. (BMI)
see Almo Music Corp.

Addax Music Co., Inc. (ASCAP)
c/o Famous Music Corp.
Att: Sidney Herman
1 Gulf & Western Plaza
New York, New York 10023

Adra Music (ASCAP)
c/o Fred Munao
175 Fifth Avenue
New York, New York 10010

List of Publishers

AGF Music Ltd. (ASCAP)
1500 Broadway, Suite 2805
New York, New York 10036

Alabama Band Music Co. (ASCAP)
803 18th Avenue S.
Nashville, Tennessee 37203

Albion Music Ltd. (ASCAP)
1706 E. 51st Street
Brooklyn, New York 11234

All Seeing Eye Music (ASCAP)
1422 West Peachtree Street, N.W.
Suite 816
Atlanta, Georgia 30309

Alley Music (BMI)
1619 Broadway, 11th Fl.
New York, New York 10019

Almo Music Corp. (ASCAP)
1416 N. La Brea Avenue
Hollywood, California 90028

Amadeus Music Co. (ASCAP)
c/o Franklin, Weinrib & Rudell
Att: Earl Rose
950 Third Avenue
New York, New York 10022

Amazement Music (BMI)
805 Moraga
Lafayette, California 94549

American Broadcasting Music, Inc.
(ASCAP)
Att: Georgett Studnicka
4151 Prospect Avenue
Hollywood, California 90027

American Compass Music Corp. (ASCAP)
see Larry Shayne Enterprises

Anidraks Music (ASCAP)
Mitchell, Silberberg & Knupp
Att: Richard I. Leher, Esq.
11377 W. Olympic Blvd.
Los Angeles, California 90064

April Music, Inc. (ASCAP)
49 E. 52nd Street
New York, New York 10022

Arista Music, Inc.
8370 Wilshire Blvd.
Beverly Hills, California 90211

Art Street Music (BMI)
c/o Fitzgerald Hartley Co.
7250 Beverly Blvd., Suite 200
Los Angeles, California 90036

Ashtray Music (BMI)
c/o Bobby Womack
2841 Firenze Place
Los Angeles, California 90046

Atlantic Music Corp. (BMI)
6124 Selma Avenue
Hollywood, California 90028

ATV Music Corp. (BMI)
c/o ATV Group
6255 Sunset Blvd.
Hollywood, California 90028

B

Ba-Ba-Do Music (ASCAP)
310 Greenwich Street, Apt. 36B
New York, New York 10013

Bangophile Music (BMI)
8033 Sunset Blvd., No. 853
Los Angeles, California 90046

Denise Barry Music (ASCAP)
c/o Peter T. Paterno, Esq.
Manatt, Phelps, Rothenberg & Tunney
11355 W. Olympic Blvd.
Los Angeles, California 90064

Beechwood Music Corp. (BMI)
6255 Sunset Blvd.
Hollywood, California 90028

Beginner Music (ASCAP)
c/o Kevin Lamb & Associates
P.O. Box 2921
Florence, Alabama 35630

Bell Boy Music (BMI)
Att: Earl Shelton
309 S. Broad Street
Philadelphia, Pennsylvania 19107

Bellamy Brothers Music (ASCAP)
P.O. Box 294
Route 2
Dade City, Florida 33525

146

John Bettis Music (ASCAP)
c/o Harley Williams
1900 Avenue of the Stars
Suite 1200
Los Angeles, California 90067

Bibo Music Publishers (ASCAP)
see Welk Music Group

Big Ears Music Inc. (ASCAP)
c/o Sy Miller
565 Fifth Avenue, Suite 1001
New York, New York 10017

Big Three Music Corp.
729 Seventh Avenue
New York, New York 10019

Big Thrilling Music (ASCAP)
see Of the Fire Music

Big Wad/Famous Music Corp. (ASCAP)
c/o Lindsey Feldman
1299 Ocean Avenue, Penthouse
Santa Monica, California 94601

Birdwing Music (ASCAP)
9255 Dearring Avenue
Chatsworth, California 91311

Stephen Bishop Music Publishing Co. (BMI)
c/o Segel & Goldman
9348 Santa Monica Blvd.
Beverly Hills, California 90210

Black Bull Music (ASCAP)
Att: Stevland Morris
4616 Magnolia Blvd.
Burbank, California 91505

Black Lion (ASCAP)
6525 Sunset Blvd., 2nd Fl.
Hollywood, California 90028

Black Stallion (ASCAP)
Strote & Whitehouse, PC
280 S. Beverly Drive
Beverly Hills, California 90212

Blackmore Music Ltd. (ASCAP)
45 E. Putnam Avenue
Greenwich, Connecticut 06830

Blackwood Music Inc. (BMI)
1350 Avenue of the Americas
23rd Fl.
New York, New York 10019

Bleu Disque Music (ASCAP)
c/o Warner Brothers Music
9000 Sunset Blvd., Penthouse
Los Angeles, California 90069

Blue Gator Music (ASCAP)
c/o Bernard Gudvit Co. Inc.
6420 Wilshire Blvd., Suite 425
Los Angeles, California 90048

Blue Lake Music (BMI)
c/o Terrace Music
818 18th Avenue, S.
Nashville, Tennessee 37203

Blue Midnight Music (ASCAP)
c/o Bug Music
6777 Hollywood Blvd., 9th Fl.
Hollywood, California 90028

Blue Network Music Inc.
Att: Dorothy A. Schwartz
c/o RCA Records
1133 Avenue of the Americas
New York, New York 10036

Blue Quill Music (ASCAP)
see Cherry Lane Music Co., Inc.

Bocephus Music Inc. (BMI)
see Singletree Music Co., Inc.

Tom Brasfield Music (ASCAP)
c/o Chris Dodson Management
3002 Blakemore Avenue
Nashville, Tennessee 37212

Brassheart Music (BMI)
c/o Jeri K. Hull, Jr.
5970 Airdrome Street
Los Angeles, California 90035

Briarpatch Music (BMI)
P.O. Box 140110
Donelson, Tennessee 37214

Bright Sky Music (ASCAP)
c/o Gursey-Schneider & Co.
10351 Santa Monica Blvd., Suite 300
Los Angeles, California 90025

Brigitte Baby Publishing (BMI)
c/o Manatt, Phelps, Rothenberg
11355 W. Olympic Blvd.
Los Angeles, California 90064

List of Publishers

Brockman Enterprises Inc. (ASCAP)
Leibren Music Division
c/o Jess S. Morgan & Co., Inc.
6420 Wilshire Blvd., 19th Fl.
Los Angeles, California 90048

Brockman Music (ASCAP)
c/o Jess S. Morgan & Co., Inc.
6420 Wilshire Blvd., 19th Fl.
Los Angeles, California 90048

Bruised Oranges (ASCAP)
c/o Sy Miller
565 Fifth Avenue, Suite 1001
New York, New York 10017

Bug Music (BMI)
Bug Music Group
6777 Hollywood Blvd., 9th Fl.
Hollywood, California 90028

Bullwhip Productions (ASCAP)
see Gedzerillo Music

Bungalow Music, N.V. (ASCAP)
Address unavailable

Bush Burnin' Music (ASCAP)
1020 Grand Concourse, Suite 17W
Bronx, New York 10451

Larry Butler Music Co. (ASCAP)
P.O. Box 121318
Nashville, Tennessee 37212

Buttermilk Sky Music (BMI)
c/o Murray Deutsch
515 Madison Avenue
New York, New York 10022

C

John Cafferty Music (BMI)
c/o Arnold Freedman
1200 Providence Hwy.
Sharon, Massachusetts 02067

Calypso Toonz (BMI)
see Irving Music Inc.

Canopy Music Inc. (ASCAP)
c/o Bruce V. Grakal
1427 Seventh Street
Santa Monica, California 90401

Captain Crystal Music (BMI)
7505 Jerez Court, No. E
Rancho La Costa, California 92008

Carbert Music Inc. (BMI)
1619 Broadway, Rm. 609
New York, New York 10019

Careers Music Inc. (ASCAP)
see Arista Music, Inc.

Casa David (ASCAP)
see Jac Music Co., Inc.

Cass County Music Co. (ASCAP)
c/o Breslauer, Jacobson & Rutman
10880 Wilshire Blvd., Suite 2110
Los Angeles, California 90024

CBS Inc. (ASCAP)
49 E. 52nd Street
New York, New York 10022

CBS Unart Catalog Inc. (BMI)
49 E. 52nd Street
New York, New York 10022

Chappell & Co., Inc. (ASCAP)
810 Seventh Avenue
New York, New York 10019

Chariscourt Ltd. (ASCAP)
see Almo Music Corp.

Chelcait Music (BMI)
6124 Selma Avenue
Hollywood, California 90028

Cherry Lane Music Co., Inc. (ASCAP)
110 Midland Avenue
Port Chester, New York 10573

Choskee Bottom Music (ASCAP)
8 Music Square W.
Nashville, Tennessee 37203

Chriswald Music (ASCAP)
6255 Sunset Blvd., Suite 1911
Hollywood, California 90028

Chrysalis Music Corp. (ASCAP)
Chrysalis Music Group
645 Madison Avenue
New York, New York 10022

Chung Music Ltd. (ASCAP)
Address unavailable

Cold Weather Music (BMI)
c/o Four Aces Music
P.O. Box 860, Cooper Sta.
New York, New York 10276

Colgems-EMI Music Inc. (ASCAP)
see Screen Gems-EMI Music Inc.

Collins Court Music, Inc. (ASCAP)
P.O. Box 121407
Nashville, Tennessee 37212

Tom Collins Music Corp. (BMI)
P.O. Box 121407
Nashville, Tennessee 37212

Combine Music Corp. (BMI)
35 Music Square, E.
Nashville, Tennessee 37203

Connie's Bank of Music (ASCAP)
c/o Fitzgerald Hartley Co.
7250 Beverly Blvd., Suite 200
Los Angeles, California 90036

Controversy Music (ASCAP)
c/o Manatt, Phelps, Rothenberg
Att: Lee Phillips
11355 W. Olympic Blvd.
Los Angeles, California 90064

Coolwell Music (ASCAP)
c/o Granite Music Corp.
6124 Selma Avenue
Los Angeles, California 90028

Copyright Control (ASCAP)
see Bug Music

Cotillion Music Inc. (BMI)
75 Rockefeller Plaza, 2nd Fl.
New York, New York 10019

Crazy Crow Music (BMI)
see Siquomb Publishing Corp.

Crazy People Music/Almo Music Corp.
(ASCAP)
c/o Mitchell Silberberg Knupp
11377 W. Olympic Blvd., Suite 900
Los Angeles, California 90064

Cricket Pie Music (ASCAP)
c/o Bug Music Group
6777 Hollywood Blvd., 9th Fl.
Hollywood, California 90028

Cross Keys Publishing Co., Inc. (ASCAP)
see Tree Publishing Co., Inc.

Billy Crystal & Paul Shaffer (ASCAP)
Address unavailable

D

Davince Music (ASCAP)
c/o Bug Music Group
6777 Hollywood Blvd., 9th Fl.
Hollywood, California 90028

Debdave Music Inc. (BMI)
P.O. Box 140110
Donnelson, Tennessee 37214

Deertrack Music (BMI)
7563 Delongpre Avenue
Los Angeles, California 90046

Del Sound Music (BMI)
c/o Happy Valley Music
1 Camp Street
Cambridge, Massachusetts 02140

Delightful Music Ltd. (BMI)
c/o Mr. Ted Eddy
200 W. 57th Street
New York, New York 10019

Deshufflin' Inc.
c/o Michael Tannen, Esq.
36 E. 61st Street
New York, New York 10021

Dorff Songs (ASCAP)
Address unavailable

Double Virgo Music (ASCAP)
c/o Mitchell, Silberberg, Knupp
11377 W. Olympic Blvd.
Los Angeles, California 90064

Dub Notes (ASCAP)
c/o Levine & Thall, PC
485 Madison Avenue
New York, New York 10022

Duck Songs (ASCAP)
P.O. Box 998
Lebanon, Tennessee 37087

Dyad Music, Ltd. (BMI)
c/o Mason & Co.
75 Rockefeller Plaza
New York, New York 10019

List of Publishers

E

Eaglewood Music (BMI)
c/o Irving Music, Inc.
1358 N. La Brea Avenue
Hollywood, California 90028

Barry Eastmond Music (ASCAP)
400 E. 17th Street
New York, New York 11226

Easy Action Music (ASCAP)
c/o Martin Cohen, Esq.
Att: Robert Destocki
6430 Sunset Blvd., Suite 1500
Los Angeles, California 90028

Eat Your Heart Out Music (BMI)
c/o Vicki Wickham
130 W. 57th Street
New York, New York 10019

Edition Sunset Publishing Inc. (ASCAP)
c/o Merit Music Corp.
9229 Sunset Blvd.
Los Angeles, California 90069

Eldorado Music Co. (BMI)
1717 N. Vine Street
Hollywood, California 90028

Edwin Ellis Music (BMI)
c/o Nurk Twins Music
1660 N. Queens Road
Los Angeles, California 90069

Elorac Music (ASCAP)
Rosenfield, Kassov & Kraus
270 N. Canon Drive, 4th Fl.
Beverly Hills, California 90210

Ensign Music Corp. (BMI)
c/o Sidney Herman
1 Gulf & Western Plaza
New York, New York 10023

Entente Music (BMI)
c/o Warner-Tamerlane Publishing Inc
9000 Sunset Blvd.
Los Angeles, California 90069

Essential Music (BMI)
c/o Law Financial Services
No. 1, Gate 6, Suite E
Sausalito, California 94965

Evansongs Ltd. (ASCAP)
c/o E.S.P. Management
1790 Broadway
New York, New York 10019

Evil Eye Music Inc. (BMI)
see Songways Service Inc.

Excalibur Lace Music (BMI)
600 Renaissance Center
Detroit, Michigan 48243

F

Fallwater Music (BMI)
see Hudson Bay Music Co.

Famous Music Corp. (ASCAP)
Gulf & Western Industries, Inc.
1 Gulf & Western Plaza
New York, New York 10023

Fate Music (ASCAP)
1046 Carol Drive
Los Angeles, California 90069

Fiddleback Music Publishing Co., Inc.
(BMI)
1270 Avenue of the Americas
New York, New York 10020

Flat Town Music (ASCAP)
Address unavailable

Fleedleedee Music (ASCAP)
c/o Jess Morgan & Co.
6420 Wilshire Blvd.
Los Angeles, California 90048

Foster Frees Music Inc. (BMI)
c/o Shankman De Blasio
185 Pier Avenue
Santa Monica, California 90405

Frozen Flame Music (ASCAP)
see Greg Guiffria Music

Funzalo Music (BMI)
225 W. 57th Street
New York, New York 10019

Fust Buzza Music, Inc. (BMI)
Att: Shari Friedman
130 W. 57th Street, Suite 11B
New York, New York 10019

G

Garden Rake Music, Inc. (BMI)
c/o Shankman De Blasio
185 Pier Avenue
Santa Monica, California 90405

Garwin Music Inc. (ASCAP)
305 E. 24th Street
New York, New York 10010

Larry Gatlin Music (BMI)
35 Music Square, E.
Nashville, Tennessee 37203

Gedzerillo Music (ASCAP)
6255 Sunset Blvd., Suite 1126
Los Angeles, California 90028

GID Music Inc. (ASCAP)
P.O. Box 120249
Nashville, Tennessee 37212

Girl Productions (ASCAP)
Address unavailable

Glory Music Co. (ASCAP)
8255 Sunset Blvd., Suite 104
Los Angeles, California 90046

Gold Horizon Music Corp. (BMI)
Columbia Plaza, E., Suite 215
Burbank, California 91505

Franne Golde Music Inc. (BMI)
c/o Rightsong Music Inc.
810 Seventh Avenue, 32nd Fl.
New York, New York 10019

Golden Bridge Music (BMI)
P.O. Box 121076
Nashville, Tennessee 37212

Golden Mountain Music Inc. (ASCAP)
c/o Freedman Snow & Co.
1092 Mount Pleasant Road
Toronto, Ontario M4P 2M6
Canada

Golden Torch Music Corp. (ASCAP)
c/o Columbia Pictures
Att: Lee Reed
Columbia Plaza
Burbank, California 91505

Goldrian Music (ASCAP)
c/o Steve Goldman
4650 Kester, No. 221
Sherman Oaks, California 91403

Bobby Goldsboro Music (ASCAP)
see House of Gold Music Inc.

Michael H. Goldsen, Inc. (ASCAP)
6124 Selma Avenue
Hollywood, California 90028

Gomace Music, Inc. (BMI)
1000 N. Doheny Drive
Los Angeles, California 90069

Gone Gator Music (ASCAP)
c/o Bernard Gudvi & Co., Inc.
6420 Wilshire Blvd., Suite 425
Los Angeles, California 90048

Granite Music Corp. (ASCAP)
6124 Selma Avenue
Hollywood, California 90028

Gratitude Sky Music, Inc. (ASCAP)
c/o Gelfand
2062 Union Street
San Francisco, California 94123

Gravity Raincoat Music (ASCAP)
see WB Music Corp.

Greg Guiffria Music (ASCAP)
222 N. Rose Street, Apt. 201
Toluca Lake, California 91505

H

Hall-Clement Publications (BMI)
see Welk Music Group

Rick Hall Music (ASCAP)
P.O. Box 2527
603 E. Avalon Avenue
Muscle Shoals, Alabama 35662

Hamstein Music (BMI)
c/o Bill Ham
P.O. Box 19647
Houston, Texas 77024

Hang Dog Music (BMI)
see Bug Music

Happy Trails (ASCAP)
6255 Sunset Blvd., Suite 1019
Hollywood, California 90028

Herald Square Music Co. (ASCAP)
see Hudson Bay Music Co.

List of Publishers

Herds of Birds Music Inc. (ASCAP)
4421 Lankershim Blvd.
North Hollywood, California 91602

Robin Hill Music (ASCAP)
511 S. Serrano Avenue, No. 601
Los Angeles, California 90020

Hilmer Music Publishing Co. (ASCAP)
see Almo Music Corp.

Himownself's Music Co. (ASCAP)
Address unavailable

Hip-Trip Music Co. (BMI)
c/o Glen E. Davis
1635 N. Cahuenga Blvd., 6th Fl.
Hollywood, California 90028

Holmes Line of Music (ASCAP)
228 W. 71st Street
New York, New York 10023

Holy Moley Music (BMI)
2114 Pico Blvd.
Santa Monica, California 90405

Hopi Sound Music (ASCAP)
c/o Chris De Walden
6255 Sunset Blvd., Suite 1911
Hollywood, California 90028

Hot Cha Music Co. (BMI)
see Six Continents Music Publishing Inc.

House of Fun Music (BMI)
c/o John Benitez
1775 Broadway
New York, New York 10019

House of Gold Music Inc.
P.O. Box 120967, Acklyn Sta.
Nashville, Tennessee 37212

House of Greed Music (ASCAP)
Address unavailable

Hudson Bay Music Co. (BMI)
1619 Broadway, Suite 906
New York, New York 10019

Huevos Rancheros Music (ASCAP)
see Bug Music

Hulex Music (BMI)
P.O. Box 819
Mill Valley, California 94942

Human Boy Music (ASCAP)
c/o Levine & Thall P.C.
485 Madison Avenue
New York, New York 10022

I

IJI (ASCAP)
c/o Chris Jasper
24 Birch Grove Drive
Armonk, New York 10540

Illegal Songs, Inc. (BMI)
c/o Beverly Martin
633 N. La Brea Avenue
Hollywood, California 90036

Index Music (ASCAP)
c/o Radall, Nadell, Fine & Weinber
1775 Broadway
New York, New York 10019

Dave Innis Music (ASCAP)
3408 Richards Street
Nashville, Tennessee 37215

Intersong, USA Inc.
c/o Chappell & Co., Inc.
810 Seventh Avenue
New York, New York 10019

Irving Music Inc. (BMI)
1358 N. La Brea
Hollywood, California 90028

Island Music (BMI)
c/o Mr. Lionel Conway
6525 Sunset Blvd.
Hollywood, California 90028

J

Jac Music Co., Inc. (ASCAP)
5253 Lankershim Blvd.
North Hollywood, California 91601

Jack & Bill Music Co. (ASCAP)
see Welk Music Group

Dick James Music Inc. (BMI)
24 Music Square, E.
Nashville, Tennessee 37203

Waylon Jennings Music (BMI)
1117 17th Avenue, S.
Nashville, Tennessee 37212

Jent Music Inc. (BMI)
P.O. Box 1566
7 N. Mountain Avenue
Montclair, New Jersey 07042

Jobete Music Co., Inc. (ASCAP)
Att: Erlinda N. Barrios
6255 Sunset Blvd., Suite 1600
Hollywood, California 90028

Joelsongs (BMI)
see April Music, Inc.

Paul Laurence Jones, III (ASCAP)
Address unavailable

Jonico Music Inc. (ASCAP)
Shubert, Silver & Rosen P.C.
316 E. 53rd Street
New York, New York 10022

Jonisongs (ASCAP)
2622 Fourth Street, Suite 10
Santa Monica, California 90405

JonoSongs (ASCAP)
2622 Fourth Street, No. 10
Santa Monica, California 90405

K

Kadoc Music (BMI)
c/o Mrs. George
702 Lenox Road
Brooklyn, New York 11203

Paul Kamanski Music (ASCAP)
see Bug Music

Kaz Music Co. (ASCAP)
P.O. Box 38
Woodstock, New York 12498

Keishmack Music (BMI)
c/o Keith Mack
127 Lexington Avenue
New York, New York 10016

King Kendrick Publishing (BMI)
Address unavailable

Kid Bird Music (BMI)
c/o Ervin Cohen & Jessup
Att: Gregg Harrison, Esq.
9401 Wilshire Blvd., 9th Fl.
Beverly Hills, California 90212

Kidada Music Inc. (BMI)
7250 Beverly Blvd., Suite 206
Los Angeles, California 90036

Kilauea Music (BMI)
c/o On Music
4162 Lankershim Blvd.
Universal City, California 91602

Don Kirshner Music Inc. (BMI)
see Blackwood Music Inc.

Know Music (ASCAP)
c/o VWC Management Inc.
13343 Bel Red Road, Suite 201
Bellevue, Washington 98005

Kortchmar Music (ASCAP)
c/o Nick M. Ben-Meir
644 N. Doheny Drive
Los Angeles, California 90069

L

A La Mode Music (ASCAP)
1236 Redondo Blvd.
Los Angeles, California 90019

Labor of Love Music (BMI)
c/o Randy Scruggs
2821 Bransford Avenue
Nashville, Tennessee 37204

Lady of the Lakes Music (ASCAP)
9845 Portola Drive
Beverly Hills, California 90210

Land of Music Publishing (ASCAP)
1136 Gateway Lane
Nashville, Tennessee 37220

Larry Junior Music (BMI)
1422 W. Peachtree Street
Atlanta, Georgia 30309

Latin Songs (ASCAP)
Address unavailable

Leeds Music Corp. (ASCAP)
c/o Mr. John McKellen
445 Park Avenue
New York, New York 10022

Legs Music, Inc. (ASCAP)
c/o Abkco Music
1700 Broadway
New York, New York 10019

List of Publishers

N. S. Leibowitz & George Feltenstein
(ASCAP)
  Address unavailable

Lido Music Inc. (BMI)
  c/o Segel & Goldman Inc.
  9348 Santa Monica Blvd.
  Beverly Hills, California 90210

Liesse Publishing (ASCAP)
  6265 Cote De Liesse, Suite 200
  Montreal, Quebec
  Canada

Lillybilly
  see Bug Music

Dennis Linde Music (BMI)
  35 Music Square E.
  Nashville, Tennessee 37203

Lionscub Music (BMI)
  c/o Michael Gesas C.P.A.
  Bash Gesas & Co.
  9401 Wilshire Blvd., No. 700
  Beverly Hills, California 90212

Lionsmate Music (ASCAP)
  see Lionscub Music

Little Diva Music (BMI)
  2029 Centry Park
  Los Angeles, California 90067

Little Doggies Productions Inc. (ASCAP)
  (Stray Notes Music Division)
  c/o Dennis Katz, Esq.
  845 Third Avenue
  New York, New York 10022

Little Mole Music (ASCAP)
  Address unavailable

A Little More Music Inc. (ASCAP)
  P.O. Box 120555
  Nashville, Tennessee 37212

Llee Corp. (BMI)
  c/o Lee V. Eastman
  39 W. 54th Street
  New York, New York 10019

Lodge Hall Music, Inc. (ASCAP)
  12 Music Circle, S.
  Nashville, Tennessee 37203

Lowery Music Co., Inc. (BMI)
  3051 Clairmont Road, N.E.
  Atlanta, Georgia 30329

M

Make Believus Music
  109 Sanders Court
  Franklin, Tennessee 37064

Makiki Publishing Co., Ltd. (ASCAP)
  9350 Wilshire Blvd., Suite 323
  Beverly Hills, California 90212

Man-Ken Music Ltd. (BMI)
  34 Pheasant Run
  Old Westbury, New York 11568

MCA, Inc. (ASCAP)
  c/o Mr. John McKellen
  445 Park Avenue
  New York, New York 10022

Mel-Bren Music Inc. (ASCAP)
  c/o Loeb & Loeb
  Att: John P. Mackey
  10100 Santa Monica Blvd.
  Suite 2200
  Los Angeles, California 90067

Midnight Magnet (ASCAP)
  P.O. Box 2678
  Beverly Hills, California 90213

Midstar Music, Inc. (BMI)
  1717 Section Road
  Cincinnati, Ohio 45237

Mijac Music (BMI)
  c/o Warner Tamerlane
  Publishing Corp.
  900 Sunset Blvd., Penthouse
  Los Angeles, California 90069

Roger Miller Music (BMI)
  c/o Burn Management Co.
  211 E. 51st Street, Suite 8E
  New York, New York 10022

Minong Music (BMI)
  P.O. Box 396
  Palos Heights, Illinois 60463

Mokajumbi (ASCAP)
  see Personal Music

Charlie Monk Music (ASCAP)
40 Music Square, E.
Nashville, Tennessee 37203

Montage Music Inc. (ASCAP)
Address unavailable

Bob Montgomery Music Inc. (ASCAP)
P.O. Box 120967
Nashville, Tennessee 37212

Moon & Stars Music (BMI)
see Cotillion Music Inc.

Moonwindow Music (ASCAP)
c/o David Ellingson
737 Latimer Road
Santa Monica, California 90402

Giorgio Moroder Publishing Co.
Att: George Naschke
4162 Lankershim Blvd.
Universal City, California 91602

Edwin H. Morris Co. (ASCAP)
see MPL Communications Inc.

Gary Morris Music (ASCAP)
Att: Gary Morris
Rt. 3
Hunting Creek Road
Franklin, Tennessee 37064

Mota Music (ASCAP)
P.O. Box 121227
Nashville, Tennessee 37212

Mount Shasta Music Inc. (BMI)
c/o Careers Music
8370 Wilshire Blvd.
Beverly Hills, California 90211

MPL Communications Inc. (ASCAP)
c/o Lee Eastman
39 W. 54th Street
New York, New York 10019

Munchkin Music (ASCAP)
Att: Frank Zappa
P.O. Box 5265
North Hollywood, California 91616

Music Corp. of America (BMI)
see MCA, Inc.

My My Music (ASCAP)
Address unavailable

My Own Music (BMI)
c/o Ellie Greenwich
315 W. 57th Street
New York, New York 10019

Mystery Man Music (BMI)
c/o Richard Wagner
414 Grenada Crescent
White Plains, New York 10603

N

NAH Music (ASCAP)
c/o Levine & Epstein
485 Madison Avenue
New York, New York 10022

National League Music (BMI)
6255 Sunset Blvd., Suite 1126
Los Angeles, California 90028

Willie Nelson Music Inc. (BMI)
225 Main Street
Danbury, Connecticut 06810

NeroPublishing (ASCAP)
505 Jocelyn Hollow Court
Nashville, Tennessee 37205

New & Used Music (ASCAP)
c/o Fischbach & Fischbach P.C.
1925 Century Park E., No. 1260
Los Angeles, California 90067

New East Music (ASCAP)
c/o The Fitzgerald Hartley Co.
7250 Beverly Blvd., Suite 200
Los Angeles, California 90036

New Generation Music (ASCAP)
Att: Gary D. Anderson
7046 Hollywood Blvd.
Hollywood, California 90028

New Hidden Valley Music Co. (ASCAP)
c/o Ernst & Whinney
1875 Century Park, E., No. 2200
Los Angeles, California 90067

New Media Music (ASCAP)
c/o Paul Tannen
1650 Broadway
New York, New York 10019

List of Publishers

New Music Group (ASCAP)
c/o Walter R. Scott
P.O. Box 1518
Studio City, California 91604

Nick-O-Val Music (ASCAP)
254 W. 72nd Street, Suite 1A
New York, New York 10023

Night River Publishing (ASCAP)
c/o Jack Tempchin
103 N. Highway 101, Apt. 1013
Encinatas, California 92024

No Ko Music (ASCAP)
c/o Bug Music Group
6777 Hollywood Blvd., 9th Fl.
Hollywood, California 90028

N2D Publishing (ASCAP)
P.O. Box 23684
Nashville, Tennessee 37202

Nurk Twins Music (BMI)
1660 N. Queens Road
Los Angeles, California 90069

Nymph Music (BMI)
90 University Place
New York, New York 10003

O

Of the Fire Music (ASCAP)
c/o Daniel Zanes
117 Pembroke Street
Boston, Massachusetts 02118

Off Backstreet Music (BMI)
90 Universal City Plaza
Universal City, California 91608

Oil Slick Music (ASCAP)
2705 Glendoer Avenue
Los Angeles, California 90027

O'Lyric Music (BMI)
c/o Jim O'Loughlin
11833 Laurelwood Drive
Studio City, California 91604

OPC (ASCAP)
c/o Buttermilk Sky Assoc.
515 Madison Avenue, Suite 1717
New York, New York 10022

Walter Orange Music (ASCAP)
see Brockman Enterprises Inc.

Otherwise Publishing (ASCAP)
c/o Mark Tanner
1009 Ninth Street, Suite 3
Santa Monica, California 90403

Oval Music Co. (BMI)
c/o Murray Wizzell
15 Central Park, W.
New York, New York 10023

P

Pacific Island Music (BMI)
see Arista Music, Inc.

Pass It On Music (ASCAP)
see Pea Pod Music

Patchwork Music (ASCAP)
c/o David Loggins
P.O. Box 120475
Nashville, Tennessee 37212

Pea Pod Music (ASCAP)
12866 Rubens Avenue
Los Angeles, California 90066

Personal Music (ASCAP)
211 W. 56th Street
New York, New York 10019

Petwolf Music (ASCAP)
1506 Dorothy Avenue
Simi Valley, California 93063

Philly World Music Co. (BMI)
2001 W. Moyamensing Avenue
Philadelphia, Pennsylvania 19145

Pink Pig Music (BMI)
c/o Funky But Music
P.O. Box 1770
Hendersonville, Tennessee 37075

Placa Music (BMI)
see Bug Music

Poisoned Brisket Music (BMI)
see Bug Music

Polifer Music (BMI)
c/o Manatt, Phelps, Rothenberg
11355 W. Olympic Blvd.
Los Angeles, California 90064

Polo Grounds Music (BMI)
Div. of David Rubinson & Friends
827 Folsom Street
San Francisco, California 94107

Postvalda Music (ASCAP)
c/o Bjerre & Miller
1800 Century Park E., No. 300
Los Angeles, California 90067

Pressed Ham Hits (ASCAP)
Address unavailable

Prince Street Music (ASCAP)
Att: John Frankenheimer, Esq.
Loeb & Loeb
10100 Santa Monica Blvd.
Suite 2200
Los Angeles, California 90046

Pullman Music (BMI)
1614 16th Avenue, S.
Nashville, Tennessee 37212

Pussy Music Ltd. (ASCAP)
Address unavailable

Pzazz Music (BMI)
see Arista Music, Inc.

Q
Queen Music Ltd. (BMI)
see Beechwood Music Corp.

R
Random Notes (ASCAP)
31 Woody Lane
Westport, Connecticut 06880

Rare Blue Music, Inc. (ASCAP)
645 Madison Avenue, 15th Fl.
New York, New York 10022

Raydiola Music (ASCAP)
P.O. Box 5270
Beverly Hills, California 90210

Ready for the World Music (BMI)
600 Renaissance Center
Detroit, Michigan 48243

Red Admiral Music Inc. (BMI)
see Chrysalis Music Corp.

Red Cloud Music Co. (ASCAP)
c/o The Fitzgerald Hartley Co.
7250 Beverly Blvd., Suite 200
Los Angeles, California 90036

Reggatta Music, Ltd.
c/o Phillips Gold & Co.
1140 Avenue of the Americas
New York, New York 10036

Reilla Music Corp. (BMI)
c/o Joseph E. Zynczak
65 W. 55th Street, No. 4G
New York, New York 10019

Revelation Music Publishing Corp. (ASCAP)
Tommy Valando Publishing Group Inc.
1270 Avenue of the Americas
Suite 2110
New York, New York 10020

Reynsong Music (BMI)
215 E. Wentworth Avenue
West St. Paul, Minnesota 55118

Rightsong Music Inc. (BMI)
see Chappell & Co., Inc.

Rilting Music Inc. (ASCAP)
see Fiddleback Music Publishing Co., Inc.

Riva Music Ltd. (ASCAP)
see Arista Music, Inc.

Rockomatic Music (BMI)
830 Warren Avenue
Venice, California 90291

Rodsongs (ASCAP)
see Kidada Music Inc.

Rude Music (BMI)
c/o Margolis Burrill & Besser
1901 Avenue of the Stars, No. 888
Los Angeles, California 90067

Rugged Music Ltd. (ASCAP)
45 E. Putnam Avenue
Greenwich, Connecticut 06830

S
Sabal Music, Inc. (ASCAP)
Att: Maggie Ward
1520 Demonbreun Street
Nashville, Tennessee 37203

List of Publishers

Carole Bayer Sager Music (BMI)
c/o Segel, Goldman & Macnow Inc.
9348 Santa Monica Blvd.
Beverly Hills, California 90210

Scarlet Moon Music (BMI)
P.O. Box 120555
Nashville, Tennessee 37212

Don Schlitz Music (ASCAP)
P.O. Box 120594
Nashville, Tennessee 37212

Screen Gems-EMI Music Inc. (BMI)
6255 Sunset Blvd., 12th Fl.
Hollywood, California 90028

Security Hogg Music (ASCAP)
c/o Ross T. Schwartz, Esq.
Att: Richard Marx
9107 Wilshire Blvd., Suite 300
Beverly Hills, California 90210

See This House Music (ASCAP)
c/o Murphy & Kress
1925 Century Park, E., Suite 920
Los Angeles, California 90067

Seesquared Music (BMI)
1266 Stanyan Street, Suite 1
San Francisco, California 94117

Larry Shayne Enterprises
6362 Hollywood Blvd., Suite 222
Hollywood, California 90028

Sheddhouse Music (ASCAP)
27 Music Circle, E.
Nashville, Tennessee 37203

Silver Angel Music Inc. (ASCAP)
c/o Franklin, Weinrib, Rudell &
Vassalo
Att: Nick Gordon
950 Third Avenue
New York, New York 10022

Sid Sim Publishing (BMI)
2112 Elder Street
Lake Charles, Louisiana 70601

Singletree Music Co., Inc. (BMI)
815 18th Avenue, S.
Nashville, Tennessee 37213

Siquomb Publishing Corp. (BMI)
c/o Segel & Goldman Inc.
9348 Santa Monica Blvd.
Beverly Hills, California 90210

Sir & Trini Music (ASCAP)
c/o Rosenfeld, Kassoy & Kraus
270 N. Canon Drive, 3rd Fl.
Beverly Hills, California 90210

Sister Fate Music (ASCAP)
c/o Cooper, Epstein & Hurewitz
9465 Wilshire Blvd.
Beverly Hills, California 90212

Six Continents Music Publishing Inc.
8304 Beverly Blvd.
Los Angeles, California 90048

Snow Music
c/o Jess Morgan & Co., Inc.
6420 Wilshire Blvd., 19th Fl.
Los Angeles, California 90048

Snowden Music (ASCAP)
344 W. 12th Street
New York, New York 10014

Soft Summer Songs (BMI)
1299 Ocean Avenue
Santa Monica, California 90401

Solidarity (ASCAP)
Address unavailable

Somerset Songs Publishing, Inc. (ASCAP)
Att: Michael Jones
1790 Broadway
New York, New York 10019

Songways Service Inc.
10 Columbus Circle, Suite 1406
New York, New York 10019

Southern Nights Music Co. (ASCAP)
35 Music Square, E.
Nashville, Tennessee 37203

Southern Soul Music (BMI)
see Tree Publishing Co., Inc.

Special Rider Music (ASCAP)
P.O. Box 860, Cooper Sta.
New York, New York 10276

Spectrum VII (ASCAP)
1635 Cahuenga Blvd., 6th Fl.
Hollywood, California 90028

Larry Spier, Inc. (ASCAP)
401 Fifth Avenue
New York, New York 10016

Bruce Springsteen Publishing (ASCAP)
c/o Jon Landau Management, Inc.
Att: Barbara Carr
136 E. 57th Street, No. 1202
New York, New York 10021

Springtime Music Inc. (BMI)
c/o Andrew Feinman
424 Madison Avenue
New York, New York 10017

Statler Brothers Music (BMI)
c/o Copyright Management Inc.
50 Music Square, W.
Nashville, Tennessee 37203

Steeple Chase Music (ASCAP)
c/o Segel and Goldman
9348 Santa Monica Blvd., Suite 306
Beverly Hills, California 90210

Billy Steinberg Music (ASCAP)
c/o Manatt, Phelps, Rothenberg &
Tunney
11355 W. Olympic Blvd.
Los Angeles, California 90064

Stone City Music (ASCAP)
c/o Gross, Shuman, Brizdle
Laub, Gilfillan P.C.
2600 Main Place Tower
Buffalo, New York 14202

Stone Diamond Music Corp. (BMI)
6255 Sunset Blvd., Suite 1600
Dept. 4-7566
Los Angeles, California 90028

Strange Euphoria Music (ASCAP)
c/o VWC Management, Inc.
Att: Ann Wilson
13343 Bel-Red Road, Suite 201
Bellevue, Washington 98005

Stray Notes Music (ASCAP)
see Little Doggies Productions Inc.

Street Talk Tunes
Manatt, Phelps, Rothenberg &
Tunney
11355 W. Olympic Blvd.
Los Angeles, California 90064

Charles Strouse Music (ASCAP)
see Big Three Music Corp.

Sweet Angel Music (ASCAP)
c/o Michael H. Goldson, Esq.
6124 Selma Avenue
Hollywood, California 90028

Sweet Baby Music (BMI)
35 Music Square E.
Nashville, Tennessee 37203

Sweet Karol Music (ASCAP)
c/o Music Umbrella
P.O. Box 1067
Santa Monica, California 90406

T

Tapadero Music (BMI)
66 Music Square W.
Nashville, Tennessee 37203

Tee Boy Music (BMI)
c/o Lipservices
263 West End Avenue
New York, New York 10023

Tee Girl Music (BMI)
c/o Lipservices
263 West End Avenue
New York, New York 10023

Temp Co. (BMI)
Att: Rochelle Mackabee
1800 N. Argyle, Suite 302A
Hollywood, California 90028

Thriller Miller Music (ASCAP)
9034 Sunset Blvd., Suite 250
Los Angeles, California 90069

Tight List Music Inc. (ASCAP)
c/o Makin Music Inc.
3002 Blakemore Avenue
Nashville, Tennessee 37212

'Til Tunes Associates (ASCAP)
c/o Symmetry Management
234 W. 56th Street
New York, New York 10019

Tionna Music
see Controversy Music

TomJon Music (BMI)
see NeroPublishing

List of Publishers

Tranquility Base Songs (ASCAP)
c/o Tom Shannon
5101 Whitesett Avenue
Studio City, California 91607

Tree Publishing Co., Inc. (BMI)
P.O. Box 1273
Nashville, Tennessee 37203

Trixie Lou Music (BMI)
14234 Grandmont
Detroit, Michigan 48227

Tuneworks Music (BMI)
5061 Woodley Avenue
Encino, California 91436

Twist & Shout Music (ASCAP)
2728 Union Street
San Francisco, California 94123

Two-Sons Music (ASCAP)
44 Music Square, W.
Nashville, Tennessee 37203

Tyrell-Mann Music Corp. (ASCAP)
Address unavailable

U

Unami Music (ASCAP)
c/o Karen G. Fairbank, Esq.
Att: Jimmy Ibbotson
1800 Avenue of the Stars, Suite 600
Los Angeles, California 90067

Uncle Ronnie's Music Co., Inc. (ASCAP)
1775 Broadway
New York, New York 10019

Unforgettable Songs (BMI)
Address unknown

Unichappell Music Inc. (BMI)
810 Seventh Avenue, 32nd Fl.
New York, New York 10019

Unicity Music, Inc. (ASCAP)
c/o MCA Music
445 Park Avenue
New York, New York 10022

Urban Noise Music (ASCAP)
251 W. 89th Street, No. 2EE
New York, New York 10024

Urge Music (BMI)
c/o Blackwood Music, Inc.
49 E. 52nd Street
New York, New York 10022

V

Virgin Music, Inc. (ASCAP)
Att: Ron Shoup
43 Perry Street
New York, New York 10014

Virgin Music Ltd. (ASCAP)
see Chappell & Co., Inc.

Viva Music, Inc. (BMI)
c/o Warner-Tamerlane
Publishing Corp.
9200 Sunset Blvd.
Los Angeles, California 90069

Jerry Vogel Music Co., Inc. (ASCAP)
501 Fifth Avenue, 15th Fl.
New York, New York 10017

W

Waifersongs Ltd. (ASCAP)
c/o Michael C. Lesser, Esq.
225 Broadway, Suite 1915
New York, New York 10007

Walk on Moon Music (ASCAP)
Address unavailable

Warner Brothers, Inc. (ASCAP)
9000 Sunset Blvd.
Los Angeles, California 90069

Warner House of Music (BMI)
9000 Sunset Blvd., Penthouse
Los Angeles, California 90069

Warner-Tamerlane Publishing Corp. (BMI)
see WB Music Corp.

WB Music Corp. (ASCAP)
c/o Warner Brothers, Inc.
Att: Leslie E. Bider
9000 Sunset Blvd., Penthouse
Los Angeles, California 90069

Web 4 Music Inc. (BMI)
2107 Faulkner Road, N.E.
Atlanta, Georgia 30324

Webo Girl Music/WB Music Corp.
(ASCAP)
c/o Rubin, Baum, Levin, Cowstant,
Friedman
645 Fifth Avenue
New York, New York 10022

Weed High Nightmare Music (BMI)
c/o Screen Gens-Emi Music, Inc.
6920 Sunset Blvd.
Hollywood, California 90028

Welbeck Music Corp. (ASCAP)
Total Video Music
c/o ATV Music Group
6255 Sunset Blvd., Suite 723
Hollywood, California 90028

Welk Music Group
1299 Ocean Avenue, Suite 800
Santa Monica, California 90401

Wenaha Music Co. (ASCAP)
P.O. Box 9245
Berkeley, California 94709

White Oak Songs (ASCAP)
see Canopy Music Inc.

Wild Gator Music (ASCAP)
see Gomace Music, Inc.

Willesden Music, Inc. (BMI)
c/o Zomba House
1348 Lexington Avenue
New York, New York 10028

Window Music Publishing Inc. (BMI)
809 18th Avenue, S.
Nashville, Tennessee 37203

World Song Publishing, Inc. (ASCAP)
c/o Chappell & Co., Inc.
810 Seventh Avenue
New York, New York 10019

Wren Music Co., Inc. (BMI)
c/o MPL Communications, Inc.
39 W. 54th Street
New York, New York 10019

Writer's Group Music (BMI)
P.O. Box 120555
Nashville, Tennessee 37212

Y

Ya D Sir Music (ASCAP)
23838 Harbor Vista Drive
Malibu, California 90265

Yellow Brick Road Music (ASCAP)
7250 Beverly Blvd.
Los Angeles, California 90036

Young Beau Music (BMI)
66 Music Square W.
Nashville, Tennessee 37203

Z

Zomba Enterprises, Inc. (BMI)
c/o Zomba House
1348 Lexington Avenue
New York, New York 10128